The J Spot

Jeané Sashi

PublishAmerica
Baltimore

© 2013 by Jeané Sashi.
All rights reserved. No part of this book may be reproduced, stored in a retrieval system or transmitted in any form or by any means without the prior written permission of the publishers, except by a reviewer who may quote brief passages in a review to be printed in a newspaper, magazine or journal.

First printing

All characters in this book are fictitious, and any resemblance to real persons, living or dead, is coincidental.

PublishAmerica has allowed this work to remain exactly as the author intended, verbatim, without editorial input.

Softcover 9781627725804
PUBLISHED BY PUBLISHAMERICA, LLLP
www.publishamerica.com
Baltimore

Printed in the United States of America

This book is dedicated to all the men and women bartenders. Continue mixing those drinks.

This book is a work of fiction. Names, characters, and incidents are the product of the author's imagination or are used fictitiously. Any resemblance to actual events, or persons, living or deceased is purely coincidental.

Edited by *Jeané Elliott Bennett & H.D. Campbell Productions*

Book Cover Design by James Lee

Acknowledgment

Thank you to N.G.J., you gave me some of my inspiration for this book that meshed with my imagination. Our conversations have been fun. Keep the conversations and the laughter flowing, that's my inspiration. You're awesome and I love you.

Much Love,

Jeané Sashi

Introduction

For months now she had been coming to this bar and sat by herself and watched the tall muscular bartender. As she sat on her usual stool and watched him, she would often think about what it would be like to have sex with him. Yes, have sex with him, for she knew that she would never be happy for life with a man like that. She just wanted him to do her wild and hard. Usually on her trip to this bar she would only drink Coke. But tonight she was drinking Jack and Coke. For it had been a week straight from hell. And the old rule of, "if it can go wrong, it will", definitely applied. So threw back her third or was it her fourth? "Ahh, who the hell cares," she thought.

She leaned forward and placed her glass on the edge of the bar so he would see it was time to refill her glass. As he approached her, he smiled broadly and she could feel his eyes take her in. Indeed his eyes scanned her low cut blue top with her cleavage classily displayed. Her long flowing dark brown hair with golden highlights seemed to shimmer under the pale lights. And her soft hazel brown eyes sparkled. Just looking at her as she sat there and smiled at him made his manhood swell.

"So you're really putting them away tonight," he said with a smile. "Care to talk about it? Everyone knows bartenders are also psychologist in a former life."

Slowly, she licked her lips and with the liquid courage of the Jack Daniels pulsing through her veins, she leaned forward pressed her breast higher with the help of her arms and the edge of the bar; gave him even more of a view. And with a soft smile and a sweet whisper, she replied, "No, I don't care to talk about it. However, I'd love to have you fuck me until I can't remember what I was upset about."

Giggled at the shocked, yet intrigued look on his face, she dipped her finger in her glass and slowly and seductively licked it clean. "So what do you say? Are you up to helping a damsel in distress?" He smiled and shook his head to clear his thoughts he leaned over the bar and kissed her passionately, he let his fingertips brush lightly over her nipples. They were hard now and pressed against the soft silk material of her top. His lips left hers he looked into her eyes and answered, "Well my dear, I will help you, what man would resist an offer like this? But, it has to be done my way. You do as you're told, no arguments and no questions. As I assure you...you will have a time you will never forget."

With a wicked smile, he asked, "so, are *you* up for it? Brave enough to dare go where you have never been?" As he took a single ice cube from her glass and ran it between her breasts before licking it.

She looked him dead in the eyes and whispered, "You lead I'll follow."

"Now you understand the game...come, his hissed reply."

He came around the bar and took her hand, and lead her to a table in the corner, he whispered in her ear as they made their way through the crowd, "Now tell me, have you ever sucked a dick in public?"

Her heart began to race and her mind screamed run...

run away, but the dampness in her panties made her stay and follow him. They reached the table he sat down and motioned for her to get on her hands and knees. Doing so, she looked up to him for guidance wondered what in the world she was going to have to do.

He took her face in his hands and kissed her once more, then directed her to get under the table. Once she had managed to get fully under the small table, she immediately saw that his dick was already free from his pants and he was stroking it.

With a snarled growl, he commanded her, "Start sucking."

Not wanting to lose the chance to screw this gorgeous creature, she did as she was told.

She began lick up and down his shaft slowly. She flicked her tongue over his balls and then ran it up to the tip. She moved her tongue in small circular motions around the head. A quick tug in her hair let her know he was not in the mood to be teased. So she sucked the swollen bulbous head of his shaft into her warm mouth and licked the precum oozing forth. Then in a quick downward motion, she has his full length deep in her throat.

She held still for a brief moment, letting him feel her throat muscles contract on his shaft, then moving her tightly pressed lips up and down his dick. Her tiny fingers moved in a swirling motion followed her lips. Her tongue flicked frantically all over every hard inch as it thrust into her mouth. Her heart was beating so fast she could hardly breathe.

The very idea of being under a table in a crowded bar sucking that awesome dick was enough in itself to make her pussy drip. Then she heard him moan and growl, "That's it you horny little girl, suck that fucking dick, show me what a good little dick sucker you are."

His words were both shocking and arousing to make her

want him to cum. She pressed her lips even tighter around his throbbing shaft and used her tongue to trace and tease every vein and wrinkle as she pumped his dick in and out of her hungry mouth and down her tight wanting throat.

She could tell he was now enjoying her mouth around his dick as his hips were now thrusting forward to meet her lips his soft moans drove her on. In her free hand, she took his balls and began to gently roll them. To her surprise, his hand covered hers and he squeezed her fingers tight. He made her clamp her hand down tightly on his heavy balls. "Like that baby do it right or I'll make you pay," he growled.

Now that she fully understood now what he wants, she decides she'll give him just what he's looking for. She squeezed his balls as tightly as her strength would allow and tugged them
   hard, out and away from his body. The hand she had on his dick began to tug harder as well...pumping his shaft without mercy.

With a wicked thought, she let her teeth graze along his entire length. His deep inhale and loud moan told her now that she was doing what he truly wanted. Suddenly his hands were wrapped in her long hair and his hips were bucking wildly out of the chair. She used all the force she could muster to slam his ass back down against the chair using nothing but her hot mouth on his pulsating dick. His body stiffened and she prepared for what she knew would be a massive load.

She slammed her mouth down fast and hard. His pubic hairs tickled her nose she held his dick deep in her throat and sucked it. In mere seconds, her mouth is filled with hot sticky wetness. His draining hard pole spews blast after powerful blast into her open throat. Swallowing as fast as she can, not wanting to waste a drop of this hard earned reward, her tongue works with her lips to continue milking him.

Once his body relaxed and she was positive he was spent, she slowly licked him clean and placed a small kiss on the head of his now, dry rod.

As she slid from under the table, she was rewarded yet again with a long deep passionate kiss and a smile. "Very good baby, you passed your first test with flying colors. Now, are you ready to go a step further?" Her mind was a blur with thoughts of,

"what could be worse than what she just did?' Little did she know that tonight her every limits would be tested.

He lead her back to the bar, he towered over her by at least a foot. She was in awe of his mere presence and in a quiet panic as to what she'd gotten herself into.

He helped her slip back onto the stool she had originally chosen to watch him from at the beginning of the night. Her blood raced through her veins so fast, she could literally feel it move through her body. Then his words rattled her to her very core.

"Now, my sweet I shall taste that sweet little pussy of yours." And without any further discussion he was between her legs on his knees. His nose nuzzled the wet spot on her panties making her quiver with both excitement and fear. "What if someone noticed? What if they were watching them right now?" She thought to herself.

As his tongue slide along the wet silk of her panties she no longer cared. "Let them all watch", she didn't give a damn. Right now her entire world revolved around wanting his tongue on her clit wanting it inside her very hot wet pussy.

Soon all her wishes were answered. He roughly yanked on her panties effectively tearing them from her body. Goosebumps rose all over her as she watched him bring them to his nose and inhaled deeply. Then tossed them to the side, he quickly set to work on her dripping slit. His tongue moved slowly and lazily up

and down the entire length of her pussy, then moving over her hard clit. Making the juices inside her drip out and dampen the barstool beneath her. His tongue seemed as if it were made of stone, it was so hard on her sensitive clit. Her body quaked as he pulled the hood back and fully exposed her big clit to the cool air and not to mention to that hot tongue of his.

He sucked her clit into his mouth he began to grind it between his teeth. Her hands held the edge of the bar so tightly, she was sure there would be nail marks in the wood. Her hips slid back which made him suck even harder to keep her clit between his skilled lips. With a chuckle he released her clit and slid his tongue down along her swollen pussy lips, as he nibbled on them and let his tongue slide between them to be able to taste the hot juices that had already begun to flow.

Her eyes slammed shut when she felt his tongue enter her, as he pumped it in and out of her tight hole, she slowly opened her eyes and was in total horror to see that a man on the other side of the bar was grinning and looking at her. She was aware that she was shaking wildly and that she was sweating even though it was quite cool in the bar. She had lost control of the loud whimpers he was extracting from her.

His tongue worked skillfully over her pussy, making it impossible for her to remain still. Her hips were thrusting forward and grinding against his face in a wild wanton way. When he took her throbbing clit between his fingers and pinched and twisted it as his tongue drilled into her sopping wet pussy, it was all she could take. Her head fell back and her eyes slammed shut. Nothing but guttural moans escaped her and she no longer cared who was watching. She was no longer able to care. Her orgasm racked her body to the deepest depths. She couldn't remember ever cumming so hard before in her entire life.

She found it hard to stay on the stool as he forced his tongue even deeper into her tight pussy wanting every ounce of juice she was now freely producing. Finally to her relief, he licked her one last time and got to his feet. He kissed her so that she could taste herself still fresh on his tongue.

He went around behind the bar and made them both a drink. He leaned on the bar from the opposite side he looked into her eyes and smiled. "So, tell me pretty lady, are you enjoying your evening so far?" She still found it hard to breathe, she simply smiled at him. He gave a deep warm chuckle and then kissed her again and allowed her time to compose herself. As he watched her intently, he played with a wayward strand of hair before tucking it behind her ear. Wickedly he smiled at her, he asked, "Just how far is the lovely lady willing to go?"

Not sure how much further he could or would push her, she smiled and nervously answered, "As far as I need to…to get what I want."

"And just what might that be my lovely little nymph?" With a new gleam in her eye, she simply answered, "To have you fuck me as hard and rough as you can."

"Ah so, I see the little lady wants to be my fuck toy. Hmmm, well, I find that most interesting. However, my shift is about over and I haven't the time required to use you properly. You return here when you feel ready to push yourself beyond everything your mind can even conger up, and I will see to it you're not disappointed."

His words made her pussy convulse, but she knew that soon, she would return and push herself past the points she never thought she could.

Warning: Hot sex in places one could never imagine, leaving the reader wanting more.

Chapter One

A quaint New Orleans Jazz Bar right off Bourbon Street. On Friday and Saturday nights the nightlife brought in all the thirty and older crowd from the working middle class. The club used to be a place where you would see older men walk in, have a few drinks, get drunk, and not walk out alone. That's right. They were picked up by a little honey and were taken to the nearest motel. Some received pleasure in the form of sex and some received pain in the form of a missing wallet. All that changed six months ago when the place was bought by a new owner, now it's more upscale. A place where people would want to come, relax, unwind and have a good time before heading to their next destination. The place is more of a New Orleans Tapas Style Bar, and Nightclub.

Modest seating and contemporary tables with warm colors painted on the walls. The lighting was dim with hues of purple. The weekends consisted of live music. Friday nights it was Jazz and Saturday nights it was Contempo Indie. The rest of the nights, the music was streamed by a computerized DJ, except Thursday nights which was Spoken Word night. Most of the Indie Poets come out on that night.

The bartender, Kevin Stokes, thirty-four, six foot four, two hundred forty-five pounds, muscular, polished attached goateé and moustaché with caramel hazel eyes that fit perfect with his milk chocolate skin and bald head. He did indeed look like a Snickers candy bar...minus the nuts. He was the epitome of a bartender and a bouncer. He ran the place, he was the Manager. He too was not sure of who the owner of this place was, he just kept it running to the letter of his job description, which was...mix drinks, tend the bar, don't put your hands in the till and make sure the customers are happy. "A happy customer is a spending customer", the company's motto.

He looked after the customer very well, especially the female customers. Kevin did have a way with the ladies. One look into those caramel eyes and they melted. He couldn't tell you how many pairs of panties he had in his office. Not that he has had sex with a lot of women, it was that the women found him so irresistibly handsome...single and married ones alike...that they leave him their panties with their business cards attached to them. Subtly is not some of these women's strong suits. Get enough drinks in some of them and they were liable to do and say anything.

Especially his latest encounter, Melanie Gray, thirty-two, single, caramel skin, hazel brown eyes, long wavy hair and from the Bayou's of Louisiana. She was the Branch Manager of one of the local banks. Living alone has its perks but it also has its disadvantages. Like tonight, she had one of the worst days that anyone can have and going home to an empty house would have been added torture for her as she had no one at home to talk to. This night she decided to stop in at her new favorite bar on this cool summer Friday evening proved to be rewarding for her and helped to get the stress of the day off her back.

Waking up in the morning started out to be a challenge for Melanie. Her alarm failed to go off. The iron was too hot for the beige print skirt she wanted to wear with her beige, pink and white blouse, which forced her to switch her outfit to wear a navy pantsuit in her moments of hurriedness and to top it off, she broke the heel on her navy Nine West pumps…all before she left her house. "Damn it, now I have to wear my new Ann Klein navy pumps. I haven't even broken them in as of yet. I hope these shits don't hurt my feet today." She complained as she stomped back out of her bedroom, barefoot with shoes in hand, "I have two meetings and I don't want to be sitting in the meetings with my shoes off." She looked down at her feet and said, "at least I'm glad I had a pedicure done yesterday." She admired the fresh raspberry nail polish on her freshly manicured less than twenty-four hour toenails.

Melanie got to the office and found that she had so many fires to put out. Two tellers called out sick, "I bet they're sick. There's a hip hop concert going on tonight. I can just bet they're shopping in the mall." She told herself after reading the messages left on her desk by her assistant Valarie. And if that wasn't the icing on the cake one of her meetings had been moved up and it was in ten minutes.

"Good Morning, Melanie," Valarie addressed her by her first name; they were informal in the bank. "The Directors are upstairs in the board room. The meeting should start in five minutes.

"Thanks Valarie. Do they know I'm here yet?" Melanie looked around her desk for her notes folder. "And where is my notes folder?"

"Yes, they know you're here and your folder is at your seat in the board room," answered Valarie. "You'd better get to running upstairs."

"Oh good, Lord, thank you." Melanie thought, "run in these shoes…never…fast walk…yes!"

All in all she had a day from hell and wanted to stop and have some eye candy while she had a drink or maybe two. Little did she know the eye candy she was going to get was not just for her eyes she smiled about her audience; she didn't mind going home that evening to an empty house. She was surprised, pleased and satisfied for now.

***

Issac Daniels, standing at six-two approximately two hundred twenty-five in weight, muscular with chestnut brown eyes and a brown low cut fade, was the other bartender that Melanie had saw in her blur of passion with Kevin, was cleaning the counter top
of bar with a smile on his face when he decided to ask what he thought was the million dollar question. "Hey Kevin man, how do you do it?" He looked at him while he stacked the doily coasters.

"Do what man? What are you talking about?" He answered while counting the liquor inventory at the bar.

"Have the women eating out of your hands and other places for that matter," both men laughed at Issac's choice of words.

"Man, I don't do anything special that they don't want me to do. They can say stop or no, but they don't. So they are ready, willing and able," he said still counting the liquor bottles, not missing a beat.

Issac stopped his straightening of the bar and looked at Kevin, "Like ole girl on the barstool tonight, she has been coming here for months and tonight it was like she was in a trance when she looked at you. She was outside of herself. She had never been that bold before…in here at least."

Kevin laughed, "I know bruh. She was off the hook and all I did was ask her if 'she cared to talk about it?' She was putting'em away tonight and she took it from there and I obliged her. She surprised me too…she took my dare."

"That's what I mean man, they're in a trance." Issac laughed again. Kevin didn't think he does not do anything special, nothing different from any other man the women just want what they want. "Kev, have you ever thought that you might get caught by the owners if they ever walked up in here?"

"Naw man, I only talk to the representative for the new owners once every two weeks. Their office is out West somewhere. They're too busy to come to 'Nawlins, as ya'll say."

"What prompted you to come to 'Nawlins from Chi-town anyway?"

"Just a change of scenery my man; change is good, sometimes and so far this change has been good." Kevin turned around from his counting and looked into a busty cleavage.

"Hi, can I get a refill on my beer?" asked the buxom female with the straight shoulder length bob hair cut with the color matching her black eyes and dark skin, holding onto her glass.

"You sure can. Tap or draft?" replied and asked Kevin, with that bartenders grin.

"MGD Lite please." responded the female not taking her eyes off Kevin as she licked her lips.

"Coming right up," Kevin stepped slightly to his left to the beer on tap.

"That's not all I'd like to see come right up," she whispered to herself.

Kevin approached her with her beer and asked, "Did you say something?"

She responded, "No, just thinking out loud." She sashayed away with her hips moving from side to side. If they moved any harder she was going to need a new hip and a new drink in her hand.

"That's what I'm talking about Kev man. She couldn't take her eyes off you. She had breast that would make a baby cry for milk...all...day...long." Stomping his foot in between words.

"Damn" in unison with Kevin.

"Baby girl definitely does have it going on, doesn't she? But, I saw the rock on her finger. I do draw my lines, man. I don't care how unhappy they are at home, not gonna touch'em. Not even flirt with them. Don't want someone's husband in my face."

"I heard that man, it's not worth it."

Kevin remembered the last time he got caught up with someone's wife. The incident landed him in jail for a period of time. He and the woman were in a hotel room not a motel room, a knock came to the door, she answered it thinking it was room service and it was her husband. He jumped on Kevin and Kevin beat the man unconscious. Charges were filed for assault and attempted murder which could have left him in prison for twenty-five years. He had a damn good attorney that got him off and when he was acquitted of all charges, he chose to leave Chi-town for a new start. If he had a PD, a Public Defender, he would have caught the case. He was thankful for the sharp shooter he had. That was when he vowed to never again mess with another married woman. Not even one that is separated who has a boyfriend, or even a B.U.D.D.Y. and friends with benefits. That shit is not ever going to happen.

Chapter Two

"This weekend went by fast. Do I remember doing anything?" Melanie asked herself over her Caramel Macchiato at Starbucks on this Sunday morning. "Oh yeah, Friday night, I was sent to heaven, or damn near heaven by that bartender. I still can't believe I did that. Oh well, no regrets." She took a sip of her hot coffee. "And I can't believe he challenged me again. Right after the first challenge. He is bold." She laughed to herself.

"Good morning. How are you lovely lady?" Issac looked down at Melanie smiling.

Melanie looked up with a surprised and shocked look on her face, with the sun in her eyes. "Hello, how are you? I'm surprised to see you?" As she was trying to shield the sun from her eyes with her hand over her Chanel sunglasses.

"I see that," responded Issac. "I won't keep you. Just thought I'd say hi. By the way, how was your head Saturday morning? I hope not too bad. You tied one on Friday night." He looked at her with a sideways grin.

"My head was okay. I did have a slight headache and a mild hangover the next morning but, for the most part, I was okay." She said as she remembered what actually took place Friday night. "I hope he doesn't think I'm a slut and that I go to bars doing what I did," she continued feeling embarrassed.

Issac said his good-byes with his Green Tea Cappuccino in his hand and left. Not once did he turn around and look back at Melanie, he just smiled to thinking. "That lady felt the sting of Kevin. Her eyes told the story. Kevin is something else."

Melanie was still seated outside of Starbucks looking at Issac as he walked away thinking, "I don't know his name or even the other bartenders name for that matter. They're both cute though. I wonder what he was thinking when he walked away."

Melanie headed back home to her domain. She was fond of her three bedroom two bath two car garage home with its nicely manicured lawn and landscaping. She worked hard to get it and she was working even harder to keep it.

When the 'For Sale' sign went up at the nightclub she was at last night she had hopes that she would be the new owner. She was going to maybe name it after her, but unfortunately she was beat out by a company out West and they changed the name to its current name. No one knew what the "J" stood for. The owners have not come out to New Orleans, they had sent contractors to remodel the place and made it look in the classy way it does. It is a nice place. "I would have never thought of a Tapas Bar. I was just going to leave it as it was; a home town bar. But it looks like the owners out West knew better. I'll just have to find another business or bar for that matter." She thought about all of that on her drive home from Starbucks, which was about ten minutes. "I should have walked and saved my gas. I can be such a lazy ass sometimes."

When she pulled up to her house, she saw someone sitting on her front porch. As she pulled into her driveway, she saw her sister Mina and then noticed that Mina had suitcases with her, "Oh hell no! What happened now?" the words fell out of her mouth loud.

"Mina, what's going on? What's with the suitcases? Where are you going?" Melanie asked knowing all too well what the answers were to her questions. Mina and her boyfriend had a fight...again. It seemed like every twenty-eight days this shit happened. "I'll be glad when they make up their minds as to what they're going to do with each other."

"Melanie, me and Charles had a fight...again." Melanie listened rolling her eyes. "And this time I've left him...for good." Mina said looking like she could bite somebody.

"Mina, you say this once a month and within two days both of ya'll are back lovey-dovey again."

"Not this time. I saw him flirting with one of the servers at that new bar, the one on the end of Bourbon Street. What's it called?" She tried to remember the name by snapping her fingers.

"The J Spot?" answered Melanie with a question, trying to help her sister with her memory.

"Yeah, The J Spot, that's it. Have you been there yet? It's been open for a little while. I hear it's nice inside, a whole lot better than it was before."

"I've been there, it's nice." Melanie said remembering Friday night. "Get your things Mina, let's go in the house." Melanie looked at Mina's luggage making a mental note to buy her sister new luggage for her next birthday present.

"You gonna help me with these?" Mina asked as she struggled with her broken down luggage.

"Nope, it's all on you." Melanie answered walking away.

"Mel, what am I going to do about me and Charles?"

"Look, you have to figure it out on your own. You guys have been going round and round for over a year. Plus, how do you know the female worked at that new spot if you haven't been there yet?"

"I was driving by and saw him and her in the parking lot. She had on the uniform I guess they wear there. He was all in her space and in her face. She wasn't pushing him away either. I saw him give her his phone number. He had the nerve to get some business cards printed with his phone number on them. He called them his calling card. Said they're for business. What kind of business he has is beyond me."

Mina dropped her bags and plopped down on the couch and sighed, "I'm done with Charles. How about we go to that place tonight and listen to some music, have a few drinks and a light dinner? I hear the food and the music there is nice. Please! I've never been there. Plus, I hear the bartenders are fine as hell!"

"Seems you've heard a lot about that place and haven't even been there. Why is that? You normally hit the new places before I do."

"I have had no one to go with all my girls are still going to the kiddie clubs. I want to go to somewhere different and grown up. I can get in there now, thirty and over, right?"

"Yes, it is. You mean none of your girls want to go check out the eye candy in there?"

"They're still chasing after bad boys. I'm done with them. I'm setting my sights on a better quality of men."

"Well, you will definitely get that there. It's more upscale, has a lot of class and the quality of people are professionals."

"Okay, can we go tonight?"

Just when Melanie thought she was going to veg out tonight and do nothing, there was Mina begging her to go with her to the one place she didn't want to see for a while. Not that she didn't like the place, it was just the bartenders sexiness unnerved her. Could she go back into the bar without wanting the bartender? Could she actually look him in the face, let alone those caramel eyes? They don't have to sit at the bar they could get a table and let someone else wait on them. Listen to the sounds of the DJ and block the bartender from her sight and her mind.

"All right, all right, stop bugging me, we can go but none of that ghetto bullshit you pull with your girls. There's a better class of men there."

"That's cool. I'm looking for a better class, anyway. None of the riff-raff I've been coming across and someone better than Charles. Out with the old, in with the new," Mina said as she waved her hand.

Mina Gray, Melanie's younger sister by two years. A Dental Hygienist by profession, she was in a relationship that was not going anywhere, although the relationship was a little over a year old, she had caught Charles cheating several times and had forgiven him each time only for him to cheat again. Plus, he couldn't seem to keep a job. Always saying he was bored with it or got fired after a few weeks because he couldn't keep his mouth shut. Nonetheless, Mina had allowed him to live with her. She was a pretty lady with hazel brown eyes and caramel skin like her sister with the same petite frame. The only difference was Mina cut her hair short. The question of the day was "why did she leave her apartment? She should have put him out."

"I'm going to take a nap. Wake me in a few hours so we can get ready for tonight," commanded Melanie as she was walking to her bedroom.

"Okay, that gives me time to do my hair and figure out what outfit I'm going to wear. I gotta be cute tonight," Mina smiled while carrying her bags into the guest bedroom.

Chapter Three

"What's up Kev, man?" Issac walked into the bar to get ready for the evening opening. Kevin was on the phone gesturing with his right hand that the person on the other end of the phone was talking too much. He was talking to the representative from the Corporate Office. The young lady was giving him some new directives for the bar. Having someone tell him what to do was not one of his strong suits. He considered himself the aggressor in all things. "Yes, I've received the new menus and have passed them on to the Chef. We see there's going to be a new menu each week starting on Sunday, ending on Saturday...that's great," Kevin said rolling his eyes to the ceiling. "Change is good, especially being in food. That breaks having the same foods over and over again," he stated to the rep. "The Chef will have all things a go for tonight. As usual, the place should be packed." With that 'good' resonates from the other end of the line along with 'good-bye' and 'have a nice evening.' Kevin hung up.

"You okay Kev, man?" Inquired Issac.

"Yeah, man, I'm okay. Just some menu changes for the Chef. The Corporate Office doesn't call often and when they do it's normally something big. The menu change is going to be good. There used to be a time when I couldn't stand change…talking about growing up a lot."

"I know what you mean man, life will do that to you whether you want to or not. So, we gonna have a good night tonight? Are you ready for the ladies?" Issac asked while he came around the bar.

"Yeah, tonight should be real nice. It's Sunday, people want to unwind before going back to work tomorrow. And about the ladies, as usual, you know they'll be dressed to impress with sexiness pouring out of their clothes…flirting with half the men in here. It's not a meat fest or watering hole but, the class of people is just that…classy." Kevin said as he still looked at the phone and wondered about the owners, his bosses.

"The DJ is getting kicked into gear. If he plays what he's practicing now, there are going to be some couples formed tonight. A lot of people won't be going home alone this evening and whatever that is coming out of the kitchen smells good." Issac said as he sniffed into the air.

"That's the new menu change for the patrons and the DJ said he wants to try something new. He wants to see how it's going to go over with this crowd." Kevin checked his cell phone that had just vibrated on his hip. He looked at the phone number on the caller I.D. and chose to ignore the call. The call was from a female he met the day he left Chicago and arrived in New Orleans. He did her the service of obliging her for an evening, now he couldn't seem to get rid of her. Just because she paid for his services and purchased a few new things for him, she thought she owned him.

When Kevin first arrived in New Orleans, he didn't have a pot to piss in, or a window to through it out of. All he had was the one hundred twenty dollars he was given when he walked out of the County Jail in Chicago. His attorney was nice enough to pay his airfare out of the Windy City; giving him a new start. Kevin stated he wanted to go someplace where no one knew him so he could have a fresh start, hence the move to New Orleans.

"Hey Issac, have you ever been out of 'Nawlins?' Traveled to other places?"

"Naw man just been planted right here in 'Nawlins. I've wanted to go out West, to Cali, to do some sightseeing but the funds hadn't been there. But, now that I have this gig and making some good money, I can take the trip when I get vacation. Why you ask?"

"I'm just asking. No particular reason. Travel is good, I think."

***

Melanie and Mina were both up trying to decide what they were going to wear to the club tonight.

Mina yelled from the spare bedroom, "Mel is this dress too short and the color too loud?" I don't want to look like I just stepped off the boulevard," Mina said and laughed at her statement. "Or maybe I should wear pants, leave something to the imagination."

"What in the hell do you have on that you have to question it so hard? If you look like a damn hooker we're staying here." Melanie yelled from her bedroom, she knew all too well she was only going because her sister wanted to go. She would rather stay at home with a book she had on her Nook that she had been dying to read by a new author named *Jeané Sashi*; she loved the title *"Intimate Moments"*; the cover caught her eye. She would rather do that than to run the gamut of facing Kevin as she recalled Friday evening again in her memory.

When Melanie entered her guest bedroom and saw the dress Mina had on, her mouth flew open. "Are you kidding me? You look like cotton candy on a caramel stick. And where did you get those shoes? Looks like you went shopping in a sex shop. Find something else to wear. The green pinstripe pantsuit you have would look nice with a pink blouse and pink shoes. That has more class to it. Plus, it would look better for where we're going."

"I didn't think about that suit and I have the perfect pink blouse and shoes. That would look better than this piece of shit ass dress that idiot Charles bought me. I'm gonna throw this damn thing along with the shoes in the trash," Mina said when she looked in the closet.

Chapter Four

The line was long, music was blaring from the doors and walls. The smells that came from the kitchen were enough to make your mouth water and stomach growl at the same time. The place was packed. Change was good.

"Can you believe it man, for a Sunday how many people have come out tonight? This is something else. And look at the ladies, you were right, dressed to impress but with class. You would have thought we had a celebrity here tonight. Hey, there's that female from Friday night. I'm surprised she showed up again so soon. I must say, she's looking real good tonight. That outfit is looking real nice on her. All her curves are showing. I didn't notice it the other night but, baby girl got a body. And the female with her is banging too. Both of them are really wearing their pants. Damn, her friend is fine, they look alike though." Issac admired Melanie and Mina as they walked in the club but had his eyes glued on Mina. Issac was looking Mina up and down drooling and Kevin walked back to his office. Issac was trying to figure out a way to get Mina's attention when a loud mouthed female barreled toward him broke him out of his stare fest.

"Where is Kevin?!" The female yelled loudly. "I wanna see him now! He's not answering my calls or calling me back.

Where is he?" She asked with her hands on her hips, rolling her neck and her eyes. "Go get him, better yet, I'll get him myself." She started to walk in the direction of the club's offices in the back.

"Whoa!" Issac said quickly as he stepped so fast that he almost jumped over the bar in front of the female. "Look, whatever it is, it's gonna have to wait. Kevin is busy. Do you see all these people around? He got a job to do and he's doing it right now, so just chill. Have a drink and sit down somewhere or better yet you can leave and I'll give him the message you were looking for him." He looked her up and down while he tried to push her towards the door. "You're dressed inappropriately. How about you go home, change your clothes and take your time doing it?"

"You're trying to get rid of me? You don't want me to see him?" asked the woman. "Is he that busy? I can see it's crowded in here."

"Girl, get out of here," Issac said as signaled for the bouncers. "Your attitude is stank and your mouth is just too loud," he said still as he pushed her towards the door.

"Alright, I'm going but, tell Kevin I was here and I want to see him," she said as she pounced towards the door. She was walking like she owned the place.

Kevin walked to the bar from the office. He was carrying a cash tray when he saw Issac and noticed the irritated look on his face. "What's up man? Who got to you? If looks could kill."

"Man, you had a loud mouth, neck rolling woman just come through here looking for you. She was a hot mess. She said she's been calling you and you haven't answered or returned her calls. Whoever the hell she is, do something with her. Fuck her and shut her ass the hell up…please!"

"Damn, that trick actually came up in here. Man, she's bugging the shit out of me. I met that trick on my flight from Chi-Town to here." Kevin reflected back on how he met the woman.

***

"Okay, this is a chance for you to start over and figure out what you're going to do with your life. Make the most of this Mr. Stokes. Hopefully our paths won't cross again," were the words of Kevin's attorney, Tony Greer when he dropped him off at the airport after picking him up once he was released from jail.

Kevin was going through the TSA Checkpoint at Chicago's O'Hare Airport when he spotted a woman having problems with her carry-on. The woman, Rhonda was on her way back home to New Orleans after spending a weekend in Chicago partying. Rhonda didn't notice Kevin had walked over to her. "I see you're having problems, need some help? You're holding up the line."

"Who gives a damn? So, either you're gonna help me pick up my shit, or get away from me," she said and hissed at him with an eat shit attitude and rolled her eyes.

"Damn, girl, you don't have to be so mean. A brotha can be a gentleman," Kevin explained while helping her pick up her mess. "Here, I think this is the last of the things that fell out of your bag. Are you straight now?" Kevin asked with an irritated look on his face.

"Yeah, that's everything. I held up the line didn't I?" Rhonda asked with an ashamed look on her face.

"It's all good," Kevin said when he walked through the metal detectors ahead of her.

Kevin made it to his airline gate just in time to board the plane, taking his seat on the plane after he put his bag in the overhead compartment. He was seated in a window seat facing another seat in front of him. Just as he was taking off his jacket, he looked up and saw Rhonda had taken the seat across from him, directly in front of him. They we're now facing one another.

"I apologize for my attitude back there, I have a bad headache. Actually, I'm hung over," she explained and laughed while she fumbled to get into her seat.

"It's cool," not really paying her any attention.

She was not bad on the eyes but Kevin's mind was elsewhere. He was thinking of finding a job and a place to live once he got to New Orleans. He had one thousand dollars on him; his attorney had given him to match the money he received from the County Jail, but he knew that was not going to last very long and to get involved with a female right now was out of the damn question. He told himself, he had to leave those wild ass females alone and have a real lady in his life… one with class. Until then now he had to get himself together.

Rhonda, sat in her seat across from Kevin, she was watching him stare out of the plane's window, and wondered what was on his mind. The air conditioner was blaring on the plane so much that she had to pull her Snuggie out of a bag she had under her seat and threw it over her body. The Snuggie covered her completely. She had already removed her shoes from her red manicured toes. Rhonda realized her height of five foot three inches was not very tall when she tried to stretch her right leg out to touch her toes to Kevin's left leg. Her toe grazed his leg which caused Kevin to break his thought process and look in her direction where she looked him in the eyes and smiled at him.

"What's up? Why are you kicking me?"

"I didn't kick you I was trying to get your attention. I can share my cover with you if you're cold." She threw her cover on his legs so it would cover them both.

***

The Snuggie was large enough for both of them sitting across from each other. Under the cover she raised her foot up his left pant leg. She rubbed her toes up and down the length of his leg, trying to reach his knee cap. She was sliding further in her seat and tried to massage his leg with her foot; all the while there were devilish thoughts that were flowing through her head. She was trying to reach his crotch with her foot. Once he sensed what she was trying to accomplish, he took hold of her foot and placed it in the center of his crotch. Much to her surprise, he was hard which she could feel through his pants and surprised at the fact that he was bold enough to make such a move. She massaged his crotch with her toes which caused his dick to become even harder to the point it felt like it was going to bust through the zipper.

Kevin became uncomfortable in his seat, he leaned forward and looked her directly in her brown blood-shot eyes, he began to have a conversation with her with his eyes, all the while fingering her pussy which was now wet with his left hand under her Snuggie as he directed her foot that was still squeezing his crotch with her toes. This caught her by surprise and she squirmed and tried to sit up in her seat. He pulled her back down and continued to flick her clit between his thumb and forefinger. The look in his eyes said, "Okay, you want to play then we'll play," He thought about taking the mile high club to a whole 'nother level.

Passengers in the other seats were looking from the corners of their eyes and wondered "what in the hell are they doing?" They saw her as she squirmed and had the look of discomfort on her face. With the sweet sexual smell that came from that corner of the plane, they realized there was some form of vaginal activity going on.

Her continued squirming made her rotate on his fingers and caused her to become wetter and her clit to become harder, while her foot was still on his crotch which he had now unzipped and her toes were now squeezing the flesh of his dick causing it to grow harder with each toe squeeze. He was also helping it along by holding her foot in place. She was on the verge of an orgasm and trying to suppress a loud scream from a strong moan. Being unable to hold the orgasm, the moan and the orgasm were let loose causing the heads of some passengers to turn away from them. Her seat was wet and he had an 'eat shit' grin on his face.

Kevin sat back in his seat and re-adjusted his pants he got back to his thoughts and looked out of the planes window.

Kevin remembered that was the day he got involved with Rhonda; a time he was trying to forget; now he couldn't get rid of her.

***

"Kev, man, what are you going to do about that woman?"

"I'll figure it out man. I know I have to do something. I gotta get rid of these damn hood-rats and do better for myself, female wise," Kevin said as he stared in Melanie's direction.

Chapter Five

"Hi can I get a Perfect 10 and a Grey Goose Lemon Drop Martini?" Mina ordered loudly, she had to raise her voice over the music to ask Issac who stood at the bar.

She and Melanie had grown tired of waiting on the waitress to come take their drink orders. Mina took the liberties to get their drinks herself, plus she wanted to get an up close look at Issac. She had been checking him out from across the room and was wondering to herself, "what's his story and if he was seeing anyone?"

While he was mixing their drinks she was really getting a good look at him; the size of his hands; the shape of his arms in his fitted short-sleeved shirt, the shape of his mouth and the color of his chestnut brown eyes. She was taking him all in as much as she could see which was from the waist up.

"Will that be all for you?" Issac asked while he still mixed her last drink.

"Yes. Oh, can we have some chips or popcorn until we decide to order dinner?"

"Sure. I'll bring your drinks and snacks over to you. I don't want you walking through this crowd with these things and have someone bump into you and spill them on you. How was that?"

"That's sweet of you, thank you. My sister and I are sitting over there," Mina replied pointing to where she and Melanie were seated.

"Cool, I'll be there in just a bit." Issac smiled which showed his left cheek dimple.

Mina sashayed back to her table with a big grin on her face she noticed Melanie was in conversation with another female. The female was so loud you could hear her a mile away. The girl was wearing a dress that left very little to the imagination and had her blond hair pulled back into a pony tail bun. As Mina approached the table she caught snippets of their conversation. The girl was going on about a man she met on a plane. He stayed with her for a minute before obtaining a job and getting on his feet. Apparently, this man moved into his own place and wanted nothing more to do with her.

"Girl, I let him stay in my apartment for three months. He found a job almost as soon as he got off the plane and starting getting back on his feet. Don't get me wrong, he paid half the rent and paid half the utilities and bought groceries but, when he decided it was time for him to leave, he left. He told me he had found an apartment for himself and he moved. He said he needed his space to collect his thoughts and continue to get himself together. Ain't that some shit? He needed his space to collect his thoughts. If you ask me, there was and is another woman." the woman stated while shaking her head. "By the way, my name is Rhonda."

"Hi Rhonda nice to meet you I'm Melanie, it sounds to me like the guy was being upfront and honest with you. He was new in town and needed to get the feel of the city and his bearing together. I really don't see anything wrong with that. Unless you two made a commitment to one another," Melanie commented with gestures of her hands.

"Naw, there was no commitment. He told me from the beginning that staying at my place would be just for a short time, but you know how we girls are? We hear what we want to hear." They stopped laughing. "But, girl, talk about lay the pipe down...he can do that. That dude would have me grabbing the sheets and calling all kinds of Jesus'. Yeah, he blew my back out. I started having feelings for him. Now, he doesn't even return my phone calls or want to see me. Could it be because I'm white?"

Melanie looked at her through shocked eyes, "I don't know. That's something you would have to ask him. I can't call it."

At that time Mina walked up, "Mel, the bartender is going to bring our drinks over to us and bring us a snack. Hi, I'm Mina," she said as she addressed Melanie and turning to introduce herself to Rhonda."

"Hi, I'm Rhonda. I like your outfit."

"Thank you."

"Min, I just met Rhonda, she's been telling me about a guy she met on an airplane. Why is the bartender bringing the drinks?"

"He didn't want me to have to walk through the crowd of people with the drinks and the snacks and risk the gamut of someone bumping into me."

"That was nice of him. Looks like he's on his way over now," Melanie looked up and saw Issac as he came towards them.

"Here you go Ladies, one Perfect 10 and one Grey Goose Lemon Drop Martini along with a basket of popcorn." He placed the drinks in front of the correct recipients and kept his eyes focused on Mina, with a smile. "If you need or want anything else, don't hesitate to let us know."

"I want a drink. I want a Gin and Juice," stated Rhonda.

"I'll get a waitress over here to take your drink order," responded Issac. He looked at Rhonda with irritation.

"Why do I have to wait on a waitress, why can't you get it, you got theirs?"

"Excuse me Miss, I'm not the waitress, I'm the bartender. Plus, I chose to do this on my own. Why am I explaining myself to you?" Issac said and walked off in the direction of the bar.

"That bartender is so rude. I came in here earlier today looking for the other bartender, the manager, and that one right there wouldn't let me see him. He claimed he was busy. He was cock blocking, that's all." Melanie and Mina looked at each other then back at Rhonda with a question mark on their faces.

"Man, that loud mouth woman that was in here earlier today looking for you, is in here. She's sitting with ole girl that you rocked the other night," Issac said informing Kevin.

"Damn, man, I don't wanna see her butt. I guess I need to face her and get it over with. I told that girl, I didn't want anything with her. She's on my nerves. And you said she's sitting with ole girl from the other night? I wonder if they know each other."

"I don't think so man, I took drinks to their table but I only took drinks to ole girl and her sister. The sister looked as though she didn't know the loud mouth."

"Cool, I'll handle her."

Chapter Six

Kevin walked over to where the Ladies were seated. "Good evening Ladies. Rhonda, can I speak with you outside for a moment?"

"Why can't we go to your office? Do we have to go outside?" Rhonda said smiling.

"Outside would be better, this way we may be able to hear ourselves talk and get away from the noise," Kevin walked towards the door leaving her trailing behind him.

Kevin reached the door and held it open for Rhonda. Once outside they walked to the parking lot under the lot light and in view of other people. Kevin realized that he had to play it safe with Rhonda, she was prone to outburst.

"What's up?" questioned Rhonda while walking up close to Kevin.

As he backed up from her Kevin plead, "Rhonda you have to stop calling me and coming to my job. There is no relationship between us. I told you this. I needed to work on me. I don't owe you anything. I even helped you with all your household expenses and even left you with some dollars. What more do you want from me? I told you all of this from the day that I met you, so you can't stand there and say you don't know any of this."

"I know you did but, I chose to ignore you and hope that you would change your mind and want a relationship with me or even more." Rhonda stood with her arms folded looking at her feet.

"Well Rhonda, I don't and you should move on. You're a pretty girl and with your sexual energy, you would have no problem getting a man. And keep dressing with all your shit hanging out, every horny ass man with a dick will be sniffing behind you."

"Okay, I get it, it is time to move on, I can do better than your sorry ass. It's all good. I thought I'd give you a chance and see if you would change your mind but I see you are standing your ground," waving her hands as she spoke.

"Thank you, yes I am. And there's no need for name calling but you're right. It's all good. If you'll excuse me I have to get back to work," he walked past her back to the club.

***

Kevin noticed there were a lot of empty seats in the packed house. Everybody was on the dance floor doing the Cupid Shuffle. He even noticed the bar area was empty as he was walking towards it. Once behind the bar he searched for Melanie. He spotted her on the dance floor with everyone else. He couldn't but help smile to himself as he watched her move. The more he saw her, he saw her in a different light, not the light he saw her in a few nights ago; he was seeing her as the lady she was. "I wonder what her story is.

What she's about? She's not like the rest of these females in here; there's an air of class about her," he thought to himself. As he looked around the club, Kevin noticed all drinks are on the tables. "Thank goodness no one is dancing with a drink in their hands," he said making a mental note of the floor.

"Man, as soon as that song came on, everyone hit the dance floor," commented Issac. "Half of these women have been trying to 'drop it' instead of 'shuffle'."

"Did anything jump off while I was outside?"

"No just the dancing. I have my eye on that cutie over there." Issac's head gestured towards Mina. "She has some class about her. I like that."

"I'm going in the office to get some paper work done. If you need for anything, come get me." Kevin then headed to his office.

Chapter Seven

Melanie's legs were sore from all the dancing she did last night. She didn't want to go to The J Spot last night but Mina had talked her into it. She was kind of glad for that. She had a good time and dancing was good exercise.

She looked at herself in the full length mirror she admired her Monday morning outfit for work. "My calves are killing me but I'm okay. That's what I get for dancing in those 4-inch BCBG's. I knew better." Looking in her shoe closet trying to decide on what shoes to wear that wouldn't pull anymore on her calves, she decided on a pair of Nine West low heels.

As she walked down the hall of her house to the front door, she looked in the guest bedroom where Mina was sleeping. "That girl could sleep through a thunder storm."

Melanie walked out of the door to her car, on her way to work. "Another day, another dollar; there has to be a better way." She thought to herself while driving.

"Good morning Melanie." Valarie handed Melanie a manila folder that contained the day's agenda.

"Good morning Valarie, how are you?" Melanie responded to her assistant.

"I'm good. Your tea and scone are on your desk. Today should be a quiet day. Your calendar is clear, there are no meetings, but we do have a teller out."

"Let me guess, Kelly again?"

"Yep," responded Valarie.

Melanie made a mental note to herself to have a talk with Kelly when and if she shows up for work tomorrow. "I have to do something about that girl."

Melanie became so engrossed in her work she didn't notice someone standing at her desk until her phone rang and she looked up to answer it. "Oh, can I help you?" she said while letting the call go to her voice mail. She looked into a pair of piercing hazel eyes and a handsomely gorgeous face.

"Yes, I need to have something reviewed on my account and the teller tells me to see you, the manager," he said as he pointed to the third teller window.

Melanie looked over his shoulder to see where he was pointing and asked him to have a seat at the same time Melanie couldn't contain the smile that has surfaced across her face. Looking at that man directly in his face and being that close to him, she couldn't believe it. "What is the problem with your account and how can I assist you?"

"There is one hundred twenty-five dollars missing from my account and I know very damn well I haven't spent any money nor have I authorized any purchases. So, I want to know where my money went." He looked her dead in her eyes without a smile.

Melanie looked at him with her head tilted, "Sir, your language and tone is not necessary. Do you have a copy of your current statement so I can go over it with you and try to figure out where the problem is?" She still managed to smile a goofy smile.

"I apologize for my language and my attitude. I just don't go for someone messing with my money. Your teller gave me a copy of my statement. I haven't looked it over yet. She just gave it to me." He was still looking serious as he handed Melanie his bank statement.

When she looked over his bank statement, Melanie read the statement line item by line item, "Mr. Stokes, I see a charge here from Fredericks of Hollywood for the amount of one hundred twenty-five dollars, it appears you ordered some items from their online store." Melanie was still smiling at him and made a mental note…"Fredericks of Hollywood, the freaks come out."

"What! Are you kidding me? I barely know how to send an email let alone know how to order online. So, you're telling me that someone used my account to order something online? How can I get my money back, I didn't order anything?"

"So, you want to dispute this charge? If so we can investigate it and find out where the transaction came from. And in the meantime, while the investigation is pending, I will have the one hundred twenty-five dollars put back into your account temporarily."

"Okay, so what does temporarily mean? Yes, I want to dispute this."

"Temporarily means that the money will be put back into your account within 24 hours while the investigation is going on. If the investigation determines you did not make the purchase, we will require the company to give you back your money and we will remove/take back the money the bank gave you. Now, if it's determined that you did make the purchase, you will have to repay the bank. So, I would suggest that you not spend this temporary replacement until this is over."

"How long will this take? I just want my money back."

"The investigation could take up to two to four weeks to

complete, if not sooner. Rest assured we'll get to the bottom of this and find where your money went."

"Thank you. Now, can I ask you another question? It's more of a personal question."

"Sure, what's your question?"

"Go out with me."

"Excuse me?"

"My bad, will you go out with me? Let me rephrase that, will you allow me to take you out? Dinner; movie; dancing; whatever you like?"

Shocked and not knowing how to answer, "You're asking me out? I'm surprised. I don't know what to say."

"Say yes. Why is this a surprise to you?"

"I mean, I know who you are and I'm just taken aback. I'm still at a loss for words."

"Don't be. Allow me to take you out and you get to know me. And I mean really get to know me, the real me. Sit down and have a real conversation with me. And me get to know you. What do you say to that?"

She stared at him as she pondered her decision, "Okay, I will go out with you," she said nervously looking down at some papers and smiled. "One question…what prompted you to ask me out? And yes, I remember the night at the club. I wasn't that drunk."

"To be perfectly straight with you, since that night I haven't been able to stop thinking about you. I saw you last night when you and that chick came in. You were looking damn good."

"That 'chick' was and is my sister. And, thank you very much."

"My bad…again. I see I have to tone down a bit. I'm not what you think I am. I'm pretty cool once you get to know me."

"What do you think I think you are?"

"I'm not sure but I'll say this, we can talk about it over dinner, deal?"

"Deal."

"On that note, I'm going to get out of here and get back to some errands before work and let you get back to your work. It was nice seeing you again, and I will most definitely be seeing you again...soon. By the way, may I have your phone number, Ms. Melanie Gray?"

"Sure," she said as she wrote her home phone number on the back of her business card.

Kevin took the business card, said his good-byes and walked out of the bank with a pep in his step and a cheesy smile across his face. He was feeling like he was on top of the world, he started singing all the way to his car.

Chapter Eight

"Mina!" yelled Melanie from her bedroom through the house. "Where are my purple shoes? And don't tell me you don't know, you called me about them this afternoon."

"I think they're in your closet, in the back, that's where I last saw them," Mina yelled back from the kitchen. "Where are you going?"

"I have a date and I want to wear those shoes with my purple and black dress."

Mina ran from the kitchen to Melanie's bedroom she asked, "A date? With whom?"

"None of your business now get out of mine," Melanie responded digging in the back of her closet. "I found my shoes, and stay out of my closet. I have it organized."

"I'll find out who he is when he picks you up. Ha!"

Little did Mina know Melanie was meeting Kevin at the restaurant, so she wouldn't get the chance to see who Melanie's date was going to be.

After she checked herself in the mirror, Melanie head out to her car. She pulled out of her driveway and got a block down the street when she received a call from Mina. "Oh, you skipped out while I was in the kitchen on the phone. That was dirty."

"Oh well, bye Mina," Melanie said and hit the off button on her phone. "She's such a dunce. She didn't look outside to see that my car was gone," she said and laughed to herself.

She arrived at the restaurant, an Italian one, she and Kevin decided upon an Italian restaurant as there are so many Cajun restaurants in the area and Italian would be something different. They both pulled up at the same time and Melanie couldn't help but think to herself, "He's on time, as a matter of fact, he's early. I'll give him brownie points for that."

"You're looking really nice tonight," Kevin addressed Melanie as he was walking over to her car.

"Thank you, you don't look so bad yourself."

Both admired each other with the first date awkwardness. "I've never been here but I hear the food is good and the atmosphere is nice," Kevin informed Melanie.

It's a nice place and yes, the food is good. I hope you do enjoy it."

They both entered the door of the restaurant, Kevin being the perfect gentleman held the door open for her. He couldn't help but check out her backside. Looking down at her round supple ample behind, the night he met her came to his mind. He thought out loud to himself, "Talk about having talent."

"Did you say something?" Melanie said turning away from the hostess after and giving her their reservation.

"Naw just thinking out loud. She's gesturing to us for our table."

Melanie sat down at the nice, cozy table that Kevin called ahead and asked for. He placed the napkin in her lap after pulling out her chair out for her to be seated. He seated himself and he looked across the table to her with a warm smile on his face, "You are really pretty. Not that I didn't notice it before but you are gorgeous. Okay, so tell me, what's your story?"

"Thank you and story? What'd you mean?"

"I mean, why are you single? That's if you're single. Please don't tell me, I'm sitting here with somebody else's woman," Kevin said and shook his head, thinking to himself, "I can't do this again."

"To put you at rest, I'm very much single and I don't have any drama. I don't like drama, bullshit or any other kind of mess. And I'm not an angry black woman. I hope that answers your question and puts your mind at ease."

Her response made him laugh, "Yes it does. I see you're about having a peaceful life; just enjoying yourself; that's cool. That's the way life should be, enjoyed. All this drama and mess is a buzz kill."

"And you, what's your story? Tell me some things about you, besides the obvious." Melanie said looking him dead in his eyes with a look that said, "You know what I mean."

"How about we order dinner and through dinner, you can find out about me. I'll answer any questions you have to the best of my ability. But I will warn you, I can be bluntly truthful and if you have a problem with pure honesty, don't ask the question."

"Okay, I can go with that. I prefer honesty, that will give me the determining factor if I want to continue dinner or not. How 'bout that?"

"Deal."

Their dinner was ordered and served. Through the course of the dinner, they found out a lot about each other. Some of Kevin's information was shocking to Melanie as she was not prepared for some of the answers. But, all in all, he was truthful.

Kevin told her he is not married and he has no kids...that he knew of. He has been up and he has be down. He has had it all and he has lost it all. He also told her about the incident that landed him in jail for a short period of time and if wasn't for the sharp shooting attorney he had, he would still be in jail facing prison time, all behind a foolish mistake he made getting involved with a married woman. A lesson he has learned from greatly.

"It's good to know you've learned from your mistakes and are moving forward with your life instead of repeating the same things over and over again. The important thing is, you realized 'how' to move forward. That's all that matters."

"That's for damn sure. I see some of the things I said didn't have you running out of here screaming. So, is that a good thing?"

"Yeah, we all make mistakes and we get through them. I'm not faulting you nor am I judging you. From what I see, you're a man that's trying to get his life back together. And in the course of it all, you like to have sexual encounters along the way." With a smile on her face, "Am I right or wrong?"

He shook his head up and down and replied smiling, "You're right. Man, you pegged me up. Good insight."

"You're not a bad man, sexy as hell but, I think you know that." Melanie gestured with a wink.

Kevin smiled back with a "Thank you."

"Are you done with dinner and dessert? That food was really good and the wine was great. I'm glad we came here."

"Yes, I am. The food here is always good."

Kevin got up to remove Melanie's napkin from her lap and help out of her chair, laid a twenty dollar bill on the table for the tip. He picked up Melanie's purse and handed it to her and proceeded to walk towards the door of the restaurant wondering what she was thinking, "yeah, he's a gentleman."

"I thought we would make it a light night and go for a

riverboat ride. We don't have to gamble, just enjoy the night air and talk some more. What do you say about that, unless you have something else in mind that you would like to do?"

"No, that's nice. Let's do it."

Chapter Nine

There was a nice breeze to the night air. The air seemed just right for the pair. The riverboat was not too crowded with gamblers and party goers. Kevin and Melanie were able to find a secluded spot on the boat where they could talk some more and enjoy each other's company without any interruptions. Waiters walked around with trays of delectable edibles and various types of drinks. Kevin was able to flag one of them down to get the both of them a drink.

"A glass of wine?" He asked of his date.

"Yes, red wine would be nice," She replied.

Kevin took the glasses of wine from the waiter's tray, he handed her drink to her looking her directly in her beautiful hazel eyes. He smiled and turned to the railing to lean over it a little. "Look how the moon is shining over the water, that's romantic. You can actually see the stars, it's like they're right here in front of you and you can touch'em. I sound like a wuss don't I? I like romance, there's nothing wrong with a man being romantic and showing his romantic side."

She took mental note of all he just said and his behavior so far through the evening made her smile even more. "No, you don't sound like a wuss. Actually, it's kind of refreshing to see a man acknowledge romance, not may do."

"I would like to be in love one day and have that feeling given back. One day it will happen. I'm not forcing it," Kevin said getting into his sensitive side.

"Are you cold?" He asked taking notice that she was putting her wrap around her shoulders and moved closer to her. He wanted to make that move earlier but he didn't want her to think that's why he asked her out.

"Just a little bit."

"Here, come here in my arms." He wrapped his large left arm around her while stepping behind her to cover his body with hers. He can now really smell the scent of her perfume and feel her entire body next to his. "Is that better?" Kevin asked with his mouth to her ear. His warm breath was on her neck, his arms were wrapped tightly around her waist and his body was pressed up against her back side.

"That feels a lot better, and I mean, feels a lot better. Your cologne, what is it?"

"It's Armani, is it bothering you?"

"No, I like it."

He relieved her glass from her hands, placed it on the railing next to his, he began to caress her fingers. Feeling her hands and the length of her fingers, Kevin noticed the length of her nails which are nicely manicured and not too long or too short. He intertwined his fingers with hers, balled both into a fist and wrapped both of their arms around her. He could feel her melting in his arms. Her head rested on the left side of his chest exposing the right side of her neck. He rubbed his nose up and down the length of her neck taking in the sweet smells of her scent. Her body relaxed more into his. He unloosened his right hand from her right hand and began to run his hand down the length of her neck. He stopped at her shoulder, which was exposed, and lightly massaged it. He was still holding on to her with his left hand, making sure she could still feel his body with hers.

The cool air had caused their bodies to become warm within each other's.

"Are you okay? Is my arm hurting you?" Kevin asked out of concern. He wanted to hear her voice; to feel the vibrations of her vocals against his chest.

"I'm okay. I'm relaxed and enjoying the night. It feels good out here. And you feel good as well."

"Thank you. Can I ask you a question?"

"Sure. What is it?"

"Can I take your wrap off and place it on the lounge chair behind us? I'd like to really have you in my arms. Is that okay with you or am I out of line?"

"I wanted to remove it. It's bunching up behind my back." Melanie removed her wrap Kevin took it from her to place it on the lounge. "That feels better. It's not that cold out anyway."

He was now in full frontal face of her, he placed a finger under her chin, lifted her head to place his lips upon hers, parting her lips with his tongue. She reciprocated with meeting his tongue with hers. Their tongues did a slow, succulent dance in each other's mouth. It was so hot in their mouths their saliva couldn't put out those fires.

When they broke from the kiss they both looked into each other's eyes a little embarrassed. They both were at a loss for words.

"I shouldn't have done that but to be perfectly honest, I couldn't help myself. You're so damn sexy. From that Friday night you came into the club, I didn't know what to say but you started it and I finished it. It wasn't about the sex but that was an added bonus, the way you walked in, sat down, your look, your conversation, you had me."

"That's a pleasant compliment. I don't know what to say. I liked the kiss, hell I loved the kiss. I didn't think I would see you outside of the club, plus I thought you were a ladies man and enjoyed all the attention you get every night."

"Well as you saw from last night. I really didn't pay attention to those ladies. I have to run that club. Most of the ladies that come in, I think are lonely in some way shape or form. I'm not there to sex serve them but you I don't know what happened. I looked at you and my dick just took over. I had to have you, I'm being honest."

Melanie laughed, "Thank you for your honesty. I couldn't believe I did what I did, and in public at that; under a table. I don't regret it. I just don't believe it happened."

Chapter Ten

As he took her by the hand he lead her over to the lounge chair, Kevin gestured for her to have a seat, "Sit back and enjoy the cruise," as he bent down in front of her, he took off her stilettos and rubbed her feet, he had the urge to kiss her pretty manicured toes but decided not to. Instead, he sat behind her straddling the lounge chair with his arms wrapped around her and his chin resting on her right shoulder with his nose pressed against her right ear. They were both looking out at the moon shining over the river water. As the moon shined lustrously over the water, he couldn't help but to kiss her on her ear. That kiss caused her to cringe. Cringe in a good way. She looked back over her shoulder at him and he kissed her on her cheek. They gave each other a sideways glance which caused the kiss on the cheek to become a full blown lip locked, tongue wagging, slurping kiss. The kiss had them both so heated, they had to break from it before something got started on that lounge chair on the riverboat.

"I hope you know I want you but I'm not going to let what happened before happen again. I have more respect for you than that. It may not seem as though, but I do. I'll say this you are good at what you do." Kevin held on to Melanie grinning. "You had my head spinning…in a good way."

"I don't know what to say. I don't behave like that, not in a public place at least but, I don't regret it one bit." Melanie replied giggling.

They sat in silence for a moment both of them were reflecting on the evening and enjoyed each other he couldn't help but let his left hand run up and down her left thigh. Feeling the softness of her silky skin, smelling the perfume scent of her hair was making his nature rise. His tongue ran up and down the back of her neck and with each stroke of his tongue, his fingers were drawing lines up and down her left thigh. She too could feel heat rise within her.

"Goodness that feels good," she spoke in a hushed tone and let out a seductive sigh. "Your hands are soft. I could let this go on for hours, but I know we have to stop it," she whispered over her left shoulder.

"Your skin is soft and I don't want to stop, but I will. I'm getting heated myself and I can feel your heat. Before I lay you down on this chaise lounge, I'd better stop." Kevin removed his hand from her thigh and smoothed her dress over the area he was caressing.

Standing up behind her, he gathered her by her waist and gently raised her up to stand. Coming around to the front of her, he knelt at her feet, lifted her right foot, placed it into her heel; followed by the left foot. He just had to do it, he couldn't resist...he kissed her on her left knee and started sucking on her kneecap which caused her legs to buckle and her to let out a moan. She had to hold his head in order to keep from falling backwards. "Oh shit! You're going to start something," she said and took a deep breath and closed her eyes.

"Ok, I'm done," she said once he realized the hardness that had crept up in his slacks. He was finding it a little difficult to stand up. "Yeah, I'm hard, let's go." Kevin took her by the hand with a sheepish grin on his face while walking to the entrance of the riverboat that had just re-entered the dock. Kevin realized he hadn't asked Melanie the important questions he needed to ask. The questions he failed to ask the first night he met and saw her; the night he had her in his sexual midst. There's no better time to ask the questions...than now.

"Can I ask you a few questions?"

"Sure."

"If I get too personal let me know, but again I can be blunt and point blank, at times."

"I gathered that. Go ahead and ask the questions. I'll answer."

"Are you married?"

"No, I'm not married." Melanie's eyebrows knitted, eyes squinted in wonder as to where that question came from. "I would not have gone out with you tonight if I were married. I'd be at home with my husband. You asked me that earlier."

"That's cool. Some people lie and their husband could be out somewhere or at work and they see that as an opportunity to step out."

"Where are you going with this question?"

"I need to know, that's all. Are you seeing someone or involved with anyone? Look, I'm not looking to get caught up in drama. You're fine and all, but it's not that serious to get caught up in someone else's mess. Know what I mean? I know I asked these questions earlier but I'm asking again for reassurance."

"I see what you mean," she said stopping in her tracks with her hands on her hips. "For the record, I will clear the air for you. I'm not married, engaged, seeing anyone, or have a B.U.D.D.Y, I'm very much single. I keep myself busy with work and occupy my free time with researching business opportunities. I want to own my own business one day. I don't do drama and I don't like drama. I don't want drama anywhere near me. So, again...I keep to myself. I hope I've answered your question or questions that you were going to ask me. Also, for the record, I've never been married and don't have children."

"Damn, girl, you didn't give me a chance to ask the questions. But, yeah, those are the questions I was gonna ask. So are you looking to have a man or just out playing because you're busy with your work and business research? A brotha would like to know. This way, you know, if we did continue to see each other, we would have to establish some ground rules. Know what I mean?"

"No, I don't know what you mean...break it down to me and not in street terms. Be real." Melanie looked at him with her head cocked to the side waiting to listen to what he had to say.

"I'm not looking to play games with anyone or to hurt anyone's feelings. In all honesty, I'm looking to make something out of my life and to have some things in life. I would like to have a lady by my side, but I know I'd have to bring something to the table. It would be nice to have someone that would work side by side with a brotha...meaning we work together to have what we want to have and accomplish the things we want to accomplish together. But, some sistas are not like that these days. They want a man with a large bank and all the extras that go along with it. Don't get me wrong, I don't mind giving to a sista but, don't look at me fo' the things I have, look at me for me. Yeah, I've been through some things with females and I don't want to go back through them. I'm not holding a grudge against women, I don't label them nor do I fault all of them for one, but I refuse to walk backwards."

"I like you. I liked you when I first saw you at the spot that Friday night. I really liked you after finding out that you're a freak and have no inhibitions," he said raising an eyebrow and smiling hard while licking his lips. "But in honesty, after tonight, spending some time with you and getting to know you a bit, I want to get to know more of you. I like your style. I saw you in your professionalism on your job, so I've seen you so far in three different lights and I like all three. Those things tell me that I want to see more, know more. If that's a problem, let me know."

Melanie smiled shyly at Kevin's words and his bluntness, "No, that's not a problem. It's doable. Now, answer me a question, who was that girl, causing a scene for your attention at the club Sunday night? No, I'm not jealous, just curious and remember I don't do drama."

"I see you were observant. You must be interested in me too," Kevin replied grinning hard.

"Stop flattering yourself and answer the question."

"She's someone I met on the plane on my flight to Nawlins'. I'll tell you the story in due time, but I'll say this, there's nothing going on between me and her. She wants it to be but, that want is not mutual. She helped a brotha out and that's it… at least in my mind but, as you saw she sees differently.

She shook her head up and down, "I can understand…look at you, you are attractive," she said as he looked at him from head to toe and back again.

"Now, that we've cleared the air on that subject, can we move on to us and see where we can go from here?" Kevin took her in his arms.

Chapter Eleven

"Girl, what is it that you want? Kevin is not here and I don't think he wants to see you. I know you have something better to do on a Friday night besides hanging around this club trying to get at a man that don't want you. You're not a bad looking chick, but you're making yourself look desperate and cheap. Look at you, you're dress is up yo' ass and what titties you have are damn near hanging out. That's not the look for this club, or have you not noticed? So I suggest you go home and change yo' clothes or better yet, just go home and don't come back." Issac shook his head in disgust.

"I take it you don't like me. That's cool but, I'm not here for you to like me and I really don't care if you have a problem with my skin color. I'm here for Kevin and he likes me and for the record, my name is Rhonda," the woman said rolling her neck.

"Girl, Rhonda, if that's what you think, you're sadly mistaken. Better yet, why am I wasting my time standing here talking to yo' trifling ass? It's obvious you don't get it, Kevin don't want you…kick rocks." Issac walked away.

***

"Good evening pretty lady. How are you tonight?" Issac complimented Mina as she sat alone at the end of the bar.

"You're alone tonight, is there something on your mind, or are you waiting on someone?" Issac was hoping that the latter was true; that she was alone.

"Hi, I'm good and you? Yeah, I'm alone, my sister is out tonight, so I thought I would come out and have a drink." Mina grinned from the inside out. "This place is nice and I like the atmosphere along with the music. You like bartending?" She was trying to keep Issac there with her tonight…"Something not too strong, I'm driving."

"How about a Cosmopolitan for the pretty lady? Not too strong and just enough to satisfy the quench."

"A Cosmo it is."

"Can I ask the pretty lady a question? If I'm out of line, please let me know."

"Ask away. What is it you want to know?"

"Are you married, divorced, single, seeing someone, involved in anyway, or have a special friend? I'm interested in seeing you and would like to know these things before I make a fool out of myself." Issac said being blunt about his intentions.

"No to all of your questions. I was seeing someone a few weeks ago but ended that recently; tired of all the drama and the mess; tired of men that say one thing and do another. Look at me, pouring out my woos on you." She giggled over her drink.

"Well, they say bartenders are also psychologists. We tend to just stand and listen," They both laughed.

"So, with you asking those questions, I'll turn those same questions around on you. How about you answering them for me?"

"That's easy…the answers are no to all of them, that's why I'm coming at you, pretty lady." He then winked at Mina before continuing. "I'm about moving forward with you… what's your sex life like?"

"You are forward…my sex life has been non-existent for the past two months, and Lawd knows a sista is feening." Mina said letting out a sigh with a wide smile. "Did I just say that? That must be the alcohol talking."

Issac looked at Mina with his left eyebrow raised and a smirk on his face. His mind is digesting the information she's just bestowed upon him, contemplating how he will be able to help Mina with her non-existent sex life. Make her feel like she has done a one-eighty from the drama she spoke about earlier. He could envision himself making love to her for hours on end with both of them panting, sweating, and grasping for air. Just the thought of that was making his nature rise. "I wonder if she can make me call her name; make me suck my thumb? I'd rather suck some other things…on her body," he laughed with that thought.

"What's so funny?"

"I was just thinking about how it would be to make love to you; sucking on parts of your body. I know I may be out of line telling you these things but it's the way I'm feeling right now. Don't get me wrong, I just don't see you for sex; I see you for me. I want to get to know you for you. Take you out for you, but making love with you would be the highlight. I'm not going to say I don't want to touch your body; that would be a lie and I ain't a liar. I want to feel every bit of it but I know in due time. That's if you allow me to. I wouldn't force you into anything.

"That's good to know. You're making me blush, I'm feeling everything you just said and I would like to see you naked.

See what you're working with," She licked her lips which had caught his full attention.

"Damn, lady, I thought you were this little quiet thing. You have a little freak in you. I like that. So, when you gonna let me take you out?" He leaned on the bar getting close up in Mina's face. Close enough where she could feel his breath on her lips.

Mina contemplated Issac's question, "When schedules permit, I guess," answered Mina. "You just want to take me out to get in my panties. You want my girl goodies," She grinned big. The alcohol was talking through Mina.

Naw, I wanna get to know you, but if I get the 'girl goodies', as you say, then so be it. I'm not going to turn the goodies down...shit." Issac licked his lips.

"So, we'll have a date real soon. I'll have to work out my work schedule, but it'll be no problem and I'll let you know what's going on. I'm serious I really want to get to know you." Issac reassured Mina of his intentions.

Chapter Twelve

Kevin was sitting in his office on the phone. Another call from the Corporate Offices, thinking to himself while listening to the female on the other end giving him directions about the bar. "Who is this woman? Is this all she does all day long is bark orders to people? She has got to be one lonely ass female." He half-listened to Nichole give him information on the happenings that was going to go on in the next few weeks. "Did she just say the owners are coming out here in the next few weeks? I don't know whether to be excited or be nervous; I've never even met or seen the owners. Or is my job in jeopardy?"

Thoughts of the shit he has done in that bar, Kevin started to remember back...

"So, this is where you work? I thought you were lying about having a job and working in a club. I thought you were one of those brothas that laid up on a woman and expected her to take care of you."

"What the fuck made you think that? Because I finger fucked you on the plane, came out here without a job and lived with you for a minute? I told you, I'm here to start over and get my shit together. If I find a woman in the process that would accept me for me and not look at me for what I don't have, that would be icing on the cake."

"Damn, I didn't mean to get you all riled up. You just don't talk about yourself a lot; so I just assumed. But, I see I made an ass out of..." she walked up close to him and got in his personal space, pressed her tits against his chest. "I'm sorry, forgive me?" She said batting her eyes.

"Don't assume shit about me, ask. If you're really sorry, show me." He took her left hand put it on his crotch, and squeezed her fingers around his dick, through his pants. "Unzip my pants and take it out."

Doing as she was told, she knelt down in front of him, took his dick in her hands and wrapped her mouth around the thick shaft. She was suck on him until he was brick hard with precum oozing from his hole. He held her by her head with her long blond hair wrapped around his fingers, held in place with his left hand and pinching her left breast nipple with his right hand. "Suck that big dick, suck it good' show me how sorry you are." All the while, the door to the club was unlocked and standing wide open, anyone could have walked in; they were in plain view.

The sound of her slurping and sucking was loud, but that didn't matter to him, he wanted what he wanted. He could be demanding when he wanted to be. He fucked her face as she sucked him to the point of explosion. He looked down and saw his cream oozing from the sides of her mouth. "Suck every bit of that shit, don't let any of it drop, swallow it all." On his orders, she swallowed it all and licking her lips as she started to come to her feet.

"See, I told you I'm sorry," she said as she looked into his eyes.

"I have done some stupid shit in the months I've been here. I wonder if the Corporate Offices have had someone out here with eyes on me," Kevin said shaking his head in his own disbelief at his actions. "Time to tighten me up; I also can't believe I crossed over the fence for a moment. That's cool for some but I'd rather not. I love my sistas." He took taking a big mental note of his past actions.

"Seeing as how the BIG bosses are coming here soon, I guess I'd better make sure this place is in great shape and looking good, not that it doesn't already. Need all "I's" dotted and all "T's" crossed. The main thing is to make sure the kitchen is doing what their supposed to be doing." Kevin walked to the kitchen to speak with the chef and his staff.

"The D.J. and the kitchen are tight as always; they better stay that way," he said walking from the kitchen back to the bar area while retrieving his cell phone from his right pants pocket.

The owners were due to arrive in the next two days, little does Kevin know. The Corporate Admin failed to give him the date…on purpose. It's not that they want to catch him in the act of doing something, they have something to tell him and want to tell him face to face. Some business is best conducted in person. The anticipation of their arrival was unnerving Kevin, he didn't know what to expect. He was wondering if he was going to be fired or if they were bringing someone else in to work with him. Issac had been grandfathered in when the new owners bought the place, as were the chef and his kitchen staff. Kevin hired the D.J. and the security.

Kevin went back to his office, sat behind the desk, looked out the window, Melaine popped in his head and a cheesy smile came across his face. Kevin had developed a big crush on Melanie. Actually, it was more than a crush. He wanted more of her and from her. Melanie could be the woman to keep him on the straight and narrow. Dialing her phone number "Hi Melanie" greeting her once he heard the sweet sound of her voice answering. This is Kevin…Kevin Stokes.

"Hi Kevin, I recognize your voice. How are you?"

Chapter Thirteen

"I see you like to have fun. For some reason I thought you were a stuck up female."

"Well, now you see, I'm not stuck up. In fact far from it."

"Having a non-traditional date with you is fun. I haven't been on a backyard picnic under a tent ever. This is fun, I like it, a simple date."

"So, tell me more about the sexy lady that's sitting crossed legged before me. I want to know all that you want to tell me. But, I'll say this I know you don't want to get hurt. I believe that's what everyone doesn't want, now, go ahead I'm listening."

"Okay, how about we do this; we ask each other one question, bouncing back and forth? I love your backyard."

The serenity of the back yard was breathtaking. The gazebo looked like something out of a romance movie with its lights and flowers surrounding the outside which played host to the padded couple's settee. The hammock that swung between two medium elm trees was just big enough to rock a couple sleeping under the stars. And not to mention the park bench surrounded by flowers and grounded flood lights with a water fountain off to the side. The backyard was so romantic.

"Thank you. I have a very creative gardner. He took some

of my ideas and ran with them. Now, don't try to get off the subject, I'm trying to get to know you, pretty lady." Issac got the conversation back on track.

"Oh, I got so lost in this yard I forgot. What is it you want to know?"

"Let's see, how about the usual common questions to start off with; favorite color, favorite foods, favorite flowers, favorite sexual position, etc., etc.?"

"Purple, chicken, daises, and you just had to ask the last one, didn't you? I don't have one...I'm open."

"Ah, freaky! I'm liking this date more and more. So, you're not so innocent after all? That's good to know."

"And, what about you, Mr. Man? The same questions back to you."

"Black, fish, don't particularly like flowers, and whatever position we're in would be my favorite. Noticed how I said 'we're'? Yeah, I'm looking to get between those thighs of yours; looking to explore you from head to toe." Issac confessed while reaching to touch Mina's left leg with his right hand.

While he explored with his hands, "You have some big pretty legs. Corn fed red bone."

Mina giggled like a schoolgirl. "I'm not that thick."

"Thick enough, I like it."

As they enjoyed their evening picnic in the backyard of his home the sexual senses for both Issac and Mina had arose.

Although the air was a little crisp tonight, if felt like summer between them. They had become so heated; they no longer had their tops on. Hands were roaming, exploring each other's bodies; tongues were dancing in mouths; they both were trying hard to catch their breaths in between kisses. It was good they were in a full tent someone would have a grass bug up her butt.

Issac gave in to the heat his body was putting out, he couldn't help but lay her down, caress her and continue kissing her in places that made her moan louder and louder. He figured he was doing something right. She held him tighter and pressed her body into his. If they got any closer, they would both wear the same skin.

"Am I out of line?" he whispered in her left ear.

"No, your hand feels good; don't stop," She answered in a hushed tone while his right hand caressed her left breast and flicked the nipple at the same time between his fingers.

"I want you, I want to make love to you but I don't want you to think differently of me. Meaning, I don't want you to think that I sex every woman that I meet...I don't and that's not a line. I'm really looking to have a lady in my life, no games. So, if that's not what you're looking for, let me know; it'll be no harm no foul, feel me?" He sat Mina up.

"Point taken. You are different. I did have you pegged all wrong. I'm glad I did...peg you wrong, that is. I'm tired of the mess I've been going through; it's time to do better for myself."

Chapter Fourteen

"I'm glad you agreed to go out with me a second time. I guess that says you're interested or you're a glutton for punishment. I'd like to think the first one is correct, so humor a brotha," Kevin smiled hard and bright at Melanie.

"You would wouldn't you? Ha-ha!"

"Oh, you gonna leave a brotha hanging like that? Okay, I'll take that and draw my own conclusion. How about that?" Kevin stuck his tongue out at her.

"Smartass. I am interested in you. If I wasn't, I wouldn't have gone out with you the first time. You're not as hard as you want to come across. There is a soft side to you. I like that side better and looking forward to getting to know it. So, yes, I'm interested…there!"

"Damn, she speaks her mind. I like, I like. In all honesty, I'm looking to slow my life down and be with just one woman. This jumping from one woman to another is not hitting on a damn thing. So, I've made the decision, that mess stops today."

"What brought you to that decision? I mean today of all days?"

At that moment Kevin's cell phone rang, was Issac.

"Excuse me I need to take this call."

"Go ahead."

"Hey man, what's up? You don't usually call me." Kevin addressed Issac with a raised eyebrow.

"Hey man, a call came from the home office, they'll be here tomorrow. What time? I'm not for sure."

"Thanks man. Glad I have everything in place. We'll be ready."

"Cool. See you tomorrow."

After he ended his conversation with Issac, Kevin turned his attention back to Melanie.

"Now to answer your question, it's not today of all days. I made this decision when I touched down in New Orleans eight months ago. Things had to change for me I couldn't keep going down the same path I was going; getting too old for that mess. Look at me baring some of my soul. It does feel good to get some of this off my chest though."

"It's good to learn more about you. You had a faraway look in your eyes when you were talking. There is more to you than women, sex and the bar. That's what I'd like to get to know… the more."

He took her into his arms, kissed her on the forehead and said, "Then you shall get to know 'the more', as you say. Come back to the club with me, I want to look over a few things."

As they walked into the club, it was business as usual and in full force. Everyone was doing their job and the patrons were happy and satisfied. Issac was doing his thing at the bar as always as were the other two bartenders and had an admirer. She looked familiar to Kevin and he was hoping he was wrong as to who she was when he and Melanie walk further into the club where the bar ended, met the restrooms and a few feet further his office was to the left. He was right the woman he saw was none other than Rhonda.

"What the hell is she doing here? Dying her hair didn't

change her looks. I'm not in the mood for bullshit or trouble tonight," He thought to himself when Issac looked up and noticed him and Melanie walking towards the office.

Issac did a head gesture towards Rhonda, Kevin pointed for Issac to come to the office. He got Melanie a seat at the opposite end of the bar and he and Issac went into the office.

"I hate to ask, what is she doing here? I don't want any trouble tonight."

"She said she came here to get out and to get over you. That wig she's wearing, I guess it's a wig, I don't know, is too much. I asked her to leave. By the way, where is that 'right to refuse sign'? We need to put it up again...like now!"

"Okay, here are five of the signs, have them put around the place but put three of them up behind the bar," He said retrieving the signs from his top desk drawer.

"Will do boss."

Both men leave the office going back to the bar area when they noticed that Rhonda had moved her seat to sit right next to Melanie. If Kevin's eyes were knives, Rhonda would have had one right in her skull.

"Girl, I'm trying to catch me a man with some dollars in his pocket. I'm not trying to work no more. You know what I mean?" Rhonda stated to Melanie over her drink.

"I guess if that works for you and that's what you want." replied Melanie.

"I wanted that sexy bartender, the one that manages the place, but he be tripping. I guess he's not into blondes or white girls for that matter, that's why I dyed my hair. I want to see the men respond to me now with my hair golden brown," Rhonda said twirling the locks of her hair.

Kevin walked up behind Melanie on her right side, kissed

her on her right ear and whispered in her ear, "You ready to go sweetie?"

Breaking from her conversation with Rhonda, "Yes, I'm ready," she answered.

"Kevin, how are you? Haven't seen you in a while; you like my hair?" Rhonda shouted over Melanie's head.

"Hi, it looks nice." He replied not looking at Rhonda and helping Melanie off the bar chair.

"I thought you prefer women with darker hair," Rhonda said as she looked straight at Melanie.

"And what the hell is that supposed to mean?" Melanie asked looking at Rhonda eye to eye.

"I'm just saying it appears he left me for you. Maybe if I had what you have, he might have stayed."

"Time for you to get your ass up out of here," Issac said pointing Rhonda to the door.

"No, let her speak, say your peace." Melanie said stopping Issac.

"Sweetie, we're leaving." Kevin grabbed Melanie around the waist to lead her to the door.

"She has something to say, let her say it." Melanie held up her hand and pulled away.

"Naw, I ain't got nothing to say. It's the alcohol talking". Rhonda picked up on Melanie's change of tone.

"Well, if that's the case, then I suggest you leave on your own accord," sternly stated Melanie.

Rhonda turned on her stiletto red heels to leave. "Oh, and by the way Kevin, you ain't shit, neither are you Mr. Bartender man," Rhonda addressed Issac.

"Don't say a word Kevin, we'll table this for later, right now I just want to enjoy the rest of this evening." Melanie then reached for her Perfect 10 drink and looked him dead in the eye to let him know she meant this is not over.

Kevin said nothing and sat down on a bar chair next to Melanie and thought to himself, "If that bitch caused me to lose Melanie, she will pay dearly." Issac went back to work behind the bar shaking his head.

Chapter Fifteen

Kevin and Issac showed up at The J Spot at ten a.m. Kevin had the plan to do some housecleaning before the owners arrived. He had summoned all the employees to be present and at their perspective stations doing housecleaning.

After four hours of cleaning the club top to bottom, both Kevin and Issac stepped onto the dance floor and looked out over the club. Both were pleased with its appearance. "They could walk through that door any minute."

"At least the place looks good." replied Kevin.

***

Lights were sparkling, the place was a buzz and people were having a good time as usual. The brunette at the end of the bar wearing the navy scoop neck dress with matching navy and cream shoes was checking out the scenery in the club and swaying to the music.

"Is the atmosphere always like this every night?" The woman asked Issac.

"Yeah, pretty much it is. Since the new owners took over and we have a new manager, this place jumps. I don't believe I've seen you in here before, I'm Issac, the head bartender and you lovely lady are…?"

"I'm Nichole, Nichole Johnson," she extended her hand to shake Issac's.

"Hello Nichole, nice to meet you."

"Nice to meet you too, Issac. So, you say you're the head bartender? Who is the Manager or does this place run itself in the evenings?"

"That would be me, Kevin, Kevin Stokes, hi nice to meet you." Kevin said as he walked into the bar area and extended his hand to shake Nichole's.

"Kevin, this is Nichole, Nichole Johnson, she's a new patron here at The J Spot."

"Again, nice to meet you Nichole; your name sounds familiar, as well does your voice," Kevin took notice.

"Hello Kevin Stokes." a very attractive milk chocolate complexioned female stepped up and extended her hand to shake his. "Nichole's name and voice should sound familiar. You've been speaking with her over the past seven months regarding this place. I'm Tonju Lowe, the owner and your boss."

"And, I'm Reggie Lowe, the second owner and Tonju's husband." He said when he extended his hand.

"Nichole is our assistant with this company and my assistant in the law firm."

Kevin's mouth was wide open with a shocked look on his face. "I don't know what to say, it's nice to finally meet all of you and to put faces to names. This is Issac he's the head bartender.

He's been here a while, before I arrived here."

"Yeah, Issac, you were grandfathered in just like the rest of the staff when we bought the place, Kevin and the DJ were the only new hires." Reggie commented.

"I like the atmosphere here Kevin. You've done a great job with the place. The people are having a great time and it's packed in here. That's a good thing. We like to see this. Kevin, what's your schedule like tomorrow at ten a.m.?" asked Tonju.

"Thank you. I believe I'm meeting with the both of you tomorrow?" Kevin answered with a quizzical question mark look on his face.

"Good answer and correction, you'll be meeting with the three of us." Reggie pointed a finger at himself, Tonju, and Nichole.

"On that note, we're going to grab a table, have dinner and enjoy the music. We'll be speaking with you tomorrow morning." Reggie cleared the way for Tonju and Nichole.

***

"Man, they snuck up on us like ghost. They must have been here for a minute and I didn't even see them and if I did, I wouldn't have known who they were." Issac wiped his brow and caught his breath, he'd been holding it through the entire course of the introductions.

"I know that's right. I was going to ask you where they come from. Mrs. Lowe is fine as hell…damn!"

"So is their assistant. She has some piercing brown eyes, and you know they're not from here. You see the stylish clothes they're wearing? That's money."

"That's the kind of money I want. I know all money ain't good money but no money is not good either. So, I want the kind of money they make. Financial independence money."

Both men start laughing with Issac stating, "Right, right!"

Chapter Sixteen

Tonju, Reggie and Nichole enjoyed their evening at their club. They knew it was doing well each month; they saw the financial statements, but they were surprised at how well. That was what prompted their visit to New Orleans, among other things.

"New Orleans is pretty. It has a culture all its own. The looks of some of these people look like they flew here from Hollywood Boulevard's nightlife. The freaks come out at night but here, it's during the day." Tonju commented with a mouthful of shrimp and grits at a small quaint southern restaurant inside the hotel.

"T, you've been eating a lot lately. Stress eating, or what's going on with you?" Reggie made a mental note through his observation of how much food Tonju had been consuming lately.

"I've noticed that also Mrs. Tonju, but I didn't want to say anything," commented Nichole.

"I don't know, I've just been extremely hungry. I don't know what it is. They say when you work out a lot your appetite increases because your metabolism is increasing. Isn't that right? Or am I wrong? I'm not stressing about anything, life is and has been good these days," replied Tonju as she looked lovingly at Reggie.

"I thought you might have been stressing about the case we're working on."

"I was thinking something else." chimed in Reggie.

"That case is a challenge Nichole, but I'm not stressing about it. And what were you thinking Reggie?" she raised an eyebrow.

Reggie remembered the night he asked Tonju to marry him...again; the night she announced that she passed the bar exam. They made good love in one of the ballrooms. But, it couldn't have been that night, he serviced her. His mind wondered to their wedding night. Oh, what a night! The entire day, for that matter was an ***intimate moment***.

Tonju hired the wedding planner of the century; she was too busy with making senior partner at the Law firm to plan it herself. The church was decorated to perfection in silver and white with sprays of pink and turquoise throughout. The venue for the cocktail party and reception were breathtaking. The colors matched that of the wedding. Tonju's wedding dress was one designed especially for her. It fit her body to perfection, hugged every curve. The shimmering white and silver mixed colors lit up the room. When she walked down the aisle, heads not only turned but mouths flew open. Men gawked and women gasped. Men were envious of Reggie and women were jealous of Tonju period. Her girls, Gisselle and Patience were right by her side all the way. Patience stood with her slightly protruding baby bump and Gisselle with her bad case of morning sickness. Gisselle and Patience both had great wedding nights and ***intimate moments*** thereafter.

The new Mr. and Mrs. Lowe for the second time around, honeymooned in Paris...as people call it, the city of love and romance. Reggie searched his mind, "Could Paris have been the place? It's been four weeks. Could it be? I hope so. I'm not going to stress her out with my guessing. I'll wait until we get back home to hit her with it, but I hope I'm right. The first time around we didn't have children, this time would be great. Everything is going so well, the business and both of our careers. I would love to hear the patter of little feet around the house."

Chapter Seventeen

"I'm glad we are able to finally meet Kevin. You may be wondering and I know you're wondering why we flew out here instead of having a conference call like we usually do. We want to talk to you about a few things regarding the club, some of the things may shock you and some may not." Tonju said starting the meeting.

"A few things have come to our attention about some of the things that have been going on here before, during, and after hours," Reggie tailgated.

"Nichole can you show Kevin the pictures?" Nichole opened a manila folder sliding it over to Kevin with a few eight by ten pictures of Kevin with females in some compromising positions.

Kevin took the photos, he looked like he was going to regurgitate and pass out at the same time. He couldn't believe what he was seeing his sex acts right before his eyes in the photos. He was wondering "Who took those pictures? When and where were they positioned in the club? Thinking again, he knew the when, just by looking at the pictures.

"Is there a problem Kevin?" Tonju asked a stunned looking Kevin.

"Who took these pictures? You've been watching me?"

"Yes, we have protected our investment. The *who* doesn't matter. What matters is, these are the one and only copies and we're turning them over to you with the negatives," stated Reggie.

"You see, we don't want them and we have no desire to do anything with them, what we want to do is make you aware of your surroundings. You never know who may be watching you."

"With that being said, Kevin, don't be alarmed or concerned you're not in any trouble nor will there be any consequences. We're adult enough to look beyond this."

"Everybody likes sex; we don't mind anyone engaging in sex, and we are aware some people are freaky, but what we do mind is someone having sex in our place of business. But, that's neither here nor there, anymore and we know it won't happen again. That's not a question."

"Kevin, as Manager, you've managed to make a success out of this establishment in the short amount of time you've been employed with Lowe Enterprises. You took our vision along with our guidance for this place and it's a place where people want to come to and enjoy themselves. We've spoken to a few of the patrons last night and they told us this is the place to be. They love this place and the atmosphere. They also stated everyone makes them feel welcomed. Not to mention the food and the music are off the hook. We're rewarding you for this accomplishment, providing you accept the reward."

"Reward? What reward? I have no idea where you're going with this," Kevin asked looking confused.

"We've bought a new club in California and we want you to run it. Meaning, you would run this one, here in New Orleans along with the one in California. You would be able to hire the staff in Cali and keep the current staff here and either hire a manager or promote from within. The choice would be yours. You would have creative freedom...meaning you'll be the General Manager of both places.

"I'm not sure but either Kevin is in shock or he just had a heart attack. Are you okay Kevin?" asked Nichole snapping her fingers at Kevin.

Kevin snapped out of his trance like he had just been slapped, "I'm...I'm okay. I'm just in shock. I don't know what to say. But, I know yes to the opportunity is my answer."

Right at that moment Kevin began to reflect on his past and all the things that he had done and been through, "God has really been smiling down on me. He has given me so many chances but none like this one. I won't blow this one," he thought to himself and realized he has never thought God was going to be good to him.

Chapter Eighteen

"So, you're moving to California? When are you leaving?" Melanie asked with a sad look on her face.

"I'll be traveling between here and there for a few weeks to a month getting the club out West together and running the one here."

"Are you going to have to move to California eventually?"

"I'm not sure. I've never been to Cali before and I'm looking forward to going, living there is one thing, but if it comes down to moving there, then so be it. I'm looking upward and forward. I would like to have you with me," Kevin said taking Melanie in his arms and kissing her neck, which caused her to giggle.

"I have a job and career here. I've worked hard to get to where I am now and I don't want to leave it. It's been a long haul but I made it happen for myself. Plus, I have a house here. My sister is here…"

Kevin put a finger to her lips and replaced the finger with a light kiss, "Your sister is grown, plus I think she'll be well occupied and taken care of. As for your house, your sister can take care of your house or you don't trust her? And, your job, hopefully you can transfer to another bank in Cali."

"You're talking like you're moving…are you? And, yes, I do trust my sister."

"I'm just making clarity if it comes down to that, I would like to have you with me...by my side. I said this before and I'm saying it again, I know it's only been a short time that we've known each other and been with each other. I feel good when I'm with you and don't want to leave you. I know that makes me sound soft but it's the truth of what I feel. It's been a long time since I've felt this way." Kevin looked Melanie directly in her eyes when he talked. "With that being said, are you willing to be with me and we work 'together' to lift each other up and get to where we both want to be? Are you game for that?" stroking the left side of her face with his right hand.

"I'm not sure what to say. There are a lot of things I'd have to consider and possibly take care of. I've been independent for so long and to change that would be a challenge. Plus, I haven't lived anywhere besides New Orleans."

"Tell me, what is it that you want Melanie? Besides to have your own business. Where do you see us going?" I mean happening between us? I've told you that I like you a lot and I'm looking for a long term relationship. I'm putting my cards on the table...face up. I really don't know what you're thinking or even know how you feel and I don't want to guess, I'd prefer for you to tell me, is that too much to ask?"

"No, it's not too much. I'm not looking for any short term relationship, I just want someone that's going to want me for me; want to be with me and only me; not tell me one thing and do some thing different; his actions are going to match his words. Are those too much to ask for?"

With that last dialogue, Kevin took Melanie in his arms, kisses her like his life was coming to an end, leaving both of them breathless.

"I guess that answered my question." Melanie came out of the kiss in a daze. "With that, my answer is...yes. I'll move with you to California, if you have to move."

Another kiss was planted on her soft, wet, luscious caramel lipstick covered lips. Kevin couldn't help but let his hands wonder over her body while locked in the kiss. He loves the way Melanie felt in his arms when he was holding her close to him. He thought, "I've found my Angel. I'm not letting her go." A smile came across his face.

"For the record, it would be nice if you wouldn't answer my questions with a question. I guess that's your 'independent' side along with a defense mechanism. I'm not out to hurt you, I've told you that, believe me."

Chapter Nineteen

"Some big changes are going to take place around here, man," Kevin informed Issac as he came around the bar.

"What's going on Kev? What happened at the meeting with the owners?" Issac asked looking puzzled.

"What do you think of this place? Be honest," Kevin asked Issac while they both looked around the club.

"I like it, man. It's cozy, warm and the atmosphere is on point. All the changes have been good changes; to the betterment of the club and the customers. What are you getting at man? You're not leaving are you? Did they fire you? Did they find out about the bullshit you've been doing in here?" This time Issac laughed heartedly but being serious."

Kevin laughed along with him, "Yeah, they found out about my sex antics, but they're overlooking those and has made me an offer that someone in my position and background can't pass up. Man, they did a background check me and read everything about my past. The kicker is, they're so down to earth, that none of my past matters what matters to them is going forward and making money. With them, the past is just that, the past." Kevin left out the part about the pictures.

"That's cool, man. So, what's the offer and is it going to affect his place?"

"To answer your questions...I'm not leaving the company, per se therefore, they didn't fire me. You'll be stepping up as manager of this place, that's if you want the job. I'll be taking the position of general manager. It appears the owners have bought a second club in Cali and have offered me the position of running this club and the one out West. I'm going out there for a couple of weeks to get that club up and running and staffed. Eventually, I may move there."

"Move there? What about your girl, Melanie? Ya'll just got together, man."

"Slow down man, thank you for thinking about my lady. She and I have had this talk, and if I do move to Cali, she's moving with me."

A surprised and shocked look was on Issac's face. "Serious? She said she'll move with you? Shit! Go on man," Issac said patting Kevin on the back. "She must really be feeling you. I ain't mad at you, man."

"So, what do you say about you becoming the manager of this spot? I know you can do it. You've been here long enough and you know better than I do at times how things run around here. There will be a pay raise, man. We'd have to hire someone to replace you, plus, your girl, Mina would like it," he said winking at Issac. "Yeah, Melanie and I have noticed how touchy, feely the both of you have gotten. To be honest, Melanie is happy to see her sister this happy. She says it's about time, but don't you hurt her, and man if you hurt her, I'm gonna get you myself."

I ain't gonna hurt her, man, I'm in love with that girl. She got a brotha open," He smiled big. "She thinks highly of you too. She's glad to see her sister smiling and not concentrating so much on work."

"Damn, in love, man? It's like that? I'm happy for you man." Kevin walked to his office and Issac walked to the liquor storage.

Chapter Twenty

Mina was lying across the couch with the ear buds to her iPod in her ears. She didn't hear, let alone see Melanie enter the front door. "Min...Min...Mina!!!" She walked over to Mina and removed the left ear bud from her ear. "Why aren't you at work?" staring down at her sister.

"The Doctor decided to close up the office early today; he wanted to start his weekend early and I didn't object...ya' feel me?" Mina said snapping her fingers.

Melanie shook her head and rolled her eyes at Mina, "Mina, move your feet so I can sit down, I need to talk to you."

"You sound serious. What's going on, and why can't you sit on the loveseat? Wait! Are you pregnant?" wrinkling her nose at Melanie.

"Girl, this is my couch", pushing Mina's feet to the floor. "And I can sit where I want to...ya' feel me? No, I'm not pregnant." She thought she could be as much as she and Kevin have been going at it. I may be moving in the next few months...three to six months, maybe. Kevin has been offered a good position from the owners of The J Spot, which means he most likely will have to move to California and I've decided to move with him."

"Whoo! What about your job at the bank? What about

your house, me, the club and Issac for that matter?" Mina got excited and now sat up on the couch.

"Calm down, Mina. About the house, you will stay here in my house. You'll pay all and I do mean all, the utilities, if you don't pay the utilities, your ass will be sitting here in the dark and I'll pay the mortgage; I want to make sure that it gets paid. Issac is going to become the new manager of the club and I've already looked into transferring to a bank branch out West, I'm just waiting to hear back, any other questions, Missy?"

Mina still looking confused, "What is Kevin going to be doing in California?"

"He's going to be the general manager of The J Spot and another club the owners just bought in California. Therefore he'll be overseeing both of them."

"Why can't he stay here and do that? This was the first one right? Why does he have to leave? People can run a business being in another state."

"You're right, and I'm not sure I think they may have plans for more businesses and may want him to be in the corporate offices to run them. Plus, he would like to go out there," Melanie answered with a question in her mind also.

"Well, change is good, and Lawd knows you are over due for some change and happiness. Since you've been dating Kevin, you've been all smiles and not burying yourself here in your office or at the bank all hours of the night and weekends. Life is too short for that. I see your groove is coming back, HEY!"

"I will say I am more relaxed and not wound so tight. It is good to have something or someone else for that matter to focus on." Melanie stared off into space with the thought of last night on her mind. ***She finally saw Kevin's small apartment. In honesty, she was thinking the apartment was*** *just the right size for the sexual escapades she and Kevin had last night. Kevin may not have had a lot of rooms in his apartment but every room was utilized to its full potential. By the time they were through, you could smell the sex throughout the apartment.*

"Mel! Snap out of it. Listen, as for me, I've forgotten all about that no good Charles. Girl, when I left work yesterday, I stopped by the mall to take back those shoes I bought; you know those multi-colored sea blue platform pumps from Nine West? Anyway, I saw Charles and I guess his new girlfriend in the mall. She was pouting because he wouldn't buy her a pair of shoes she wanted. Girl, Melanie, I broke out laughing, that girl was actually pouting and saying, "I thought you had money, you have that nice apartment." It took all that I had in me not to go over to them and bust his bubble. I couldn't stop laughing." Mina laughed so hard, she was bent over. "Girl, he still has no job and the girl went on to say that the utilities are getting shut off, neither one of them works. When he spotted me, he started walking towards me and I started walking away...fast." Both Mina and Melanie laughed hysterically until tears were rolling down their faces.

"It's good you got away from him when you did. I hate to put the brotha down but he seemed lazy to me and has no drive nor ambition. Let him continue to be someone else's problem, you're going forward."

Chapter Twenty-One

It seemed as though the days and nights were getting longer, or was it that Kevin was just anxious for the next phase of his life to start. Back in Chicago, it seemed he couldn't catch a break. He was not uneducated he actually had a Bachelor's Degree in Business. It was just the job market had become so scarce that he started working odd jobs and doing what he had to do to make ends meet. For some reason the ends weren't meeting, not until he came across that married woman. He became somewhat of a kept man. She was doing and buying everything for him. He had no worries until she became demanding. That was when the bottom started to fall out. Kevin didn't and still doesn't like a woman being too demanding, especially where he is concerned. He stands firm about the man wearing the pants and being in charge. He will allow the woman some room.

He tried to end things with her and she became demanding about the things she had done for him. He told her, he would give her everything back and just walk away, but she told him to keep the clothes, the jewelry, the furnished apartment, and the car, all she wanted was one last roll in the hay with him. She wanted to feel his manliness inside of her one last time and she would leave him alone. She knew that was a lie and so did he.

Kevin decided to oblige her, plus he was never one to turn down sex. He went to the hotel where they always met; the same floor, the same room; she always left the room key under the door mat for him. This particular day, Kevin went in as usual and as usual she wasted no time for garments. The lady was sprawled out across the executive king sized bed bare ass naked. There was nothing to be left to the imagination.

Breasts were hanging and pussy was dripping wet. He walked in and saw her with her fingers playing with herself that sight only made his dick dance in his pants. If it could have come out on its own, it would have opened up the zipper and attacked her. At the sight of her, Kevin started to undress and walked towards the bed at the same time. By the time he had reached the head of the bed where her head laid on the pillow, he was fully undressed with a rock hard dick leading the way. She wasted no time. She knew exactly what to do with his shaft and knew to give it the attention it wanted and needed. She took it down her throat like it was the last piece of sausage in the building. She kneaded and massaged his balls as if they were her own personal stress balls. Kevin had to put his left hand on the wall to keep his balance while he grabbed her hair with his right hand. She sucked him, he moaned and rocked. He rocked himself into an explosion. He came so hard, he saw stars. Juices were running from the sides of her mouth as she swallowed what was in her throat. Just as he let loose of her hair and was reaching for her left breast, a knock came at the door. She released his manhood, "I ordered us room service," she said with a devilish grin. "I'll get it." She go up and sashayed to the door...naked.

She opened the door and much to her surprise, it was her husband.

Chapter Twenty-Two

The club was jumping tonight. There were wall to wall people everywhere. The chef must really be on his j-o-b tonight, people were smacking their lips and licking their fingers all the while swaying in their seats to the tunes the D.J. was dropping down.

Kevin had the chef change the menu this Sunday evening. The change to gumbo, crawfish étoufeé, jambalaya, hush puppies, blazin' hot wings, crab cakes, and a boat load of other delectable edibles were making the customers very happy. Melanie and Mina came through the door at the right time, "Hey, now, that's what I'm talkin' bout," yelled Mina headed straight for the dance floor as she grabbed Melanie's hand pulling her with her. The D.J. just dropped Superstarvic rapping The Wobble everybody was up on the dance floor doing the Wobble. All seats were empty. Melanie was enjoying herself so much she didn't realize Kevin was behind her, most definitely doing wobbling, when she felt hands on her waist causing her to lose her step from the surprise. He danced up close to her that the wobble became a grind on the dance floor.

Kevin turned Melanie around to face him, took her in his arms and planted a kiss on her as if no one in the place was there. That kiss had Kevin questioning himself regarding his feelings for Melanie. He knew he liked her...a lot, wanted to be with her, but love? He wasn't sure of that emotion. That was an emotion he hadn't felt in years. An emotion he tried to keep buried. It looked like it was coming to surface. "Should I fight it or should I just let it happen?" He thought to himself. "Too late, I think it's already happened." He believed, shaking his head and smiling.

He took Melanie by the hand and led her off the dance floor to his office. Once inside the medium sized office where the lights were turned down low as Kevin kept them when he was out of the office in the club area. The ambiance was perfect for the way Kevin was feeling towards Melanie at that moment. Kissing her again with all the passion he had stored in him causing his nature to rise. He walked her backwards to a settee sofa he had at the far right wall in his office next to an end table hosting a soft lit lamp with a rust colored shade. He sat her down, not breaking their kiss he whispered in between breaths, "I have something for you." With that statement, Kevin slides his hands up Melanie's thighs, under her dress, to the top of her beige lace thong. He began to pull them down with a little help from her raising her butt off the sofa and her girl goodies exactly where he wanted them...in his face.

He barely got her thong off her when he started to devour her. He attacked her womanhood as if his life were dependent on it, sending waves through her body, causing her to moan loudly. "I told you I had something for you," He looked up at her while still giving her a tongue lashing and not missing a beat. All the while Melanie was cupping his head like she was holding on for dear life. She could feel an explosion brewing inside her. Her volcano was about to erupt; the eruption and a scream come together causing her to collapse back on the sofa with a wide grin on her beautiful glowing face.

Kevin came up for air, gently kissed her on her breathless lips, "Hello beautiful lady."

Melanie out of breath responded, "Hiii!"

Chapter Twenty-Three

"In two weeks, I take over as manager of the club. I still can't believe it. I've been there three years and was never sure if there was advancement potential, so I just became comfortable with being the bartender...at least I had a job. The tips were good and it paid the bills. If afforded me to be able to buy my house, so I was cool with it all, but now this? Wow, I'm still feeling amazed. I have only Kevin to thank for this. If he hadn't come here, I don't know if this would be happening. He really turned this place around and made it happen." Issac exclaimed while lying in bed with Mina engaging in pillow talk.

"I like to see you smile. You're cute." Mina stroked the left side of Issac's face. There's no other place to go from here than up."

"I'd like to have you by my side, that's if you want to be there. Better yet, we're by each other's side pulling each other up. For every good man, there is a good woman with him." Issac winked at Mina.

"I'm not going anywhere. Since I've met you, I've changed some things in life all for the better."

***

Kevin looked around his tiny apartment deciding where to

start with his packing. He didn't have much, pretty much the clothes on his back and clothes he had acquired since he had been in New Orleans.

"I should just close up this apartment and turn over the keys. I won't need it anymore with traveling back and forth I can get a hotel room in both places," Kevin thought to himself.

He was startled from his thought by the ringing of his phone. He answered the phone through his Bluetooth.

"Hello?"

"Hey You. Did I catch you at a bad time?" asked Melanie.

"Hey Babe, no you didn't, I was just deep in thought about this place and the new job. What's going on with you?"

"Well, I just got word that there is an opening for a branch manager at one of our branches in California. I had a telephone interview this morning with the bank V.P. and I have another interview with Personnel tomorrow…so, we'll see the outcome. I feel pretty positive."

"That's great, now are you ready to start packing?"

"There's not much for me to pack besides clothes, Mina will be staying here in the house."

"Babe, I've seen your closet, it will fill up and entire house. So, you're telling me, we're going to be traveling like Imelda Marcos? Woman, will the airport be able to handle it?"

"Airport? I thought we were driving? What are we going to do about transportation there? I hear traffic there is awful but we'll need our cars."

"Calm down, pretty lady. We will have our cars. We will rent a car when we first get there and come back to New Orleans to drive our cars back to Cali, fair enough?"

"Fair enough so, I'll leave some of my things here. We can get them when we come back and Mina can mail some things to me."

"Cool."

Chapter Twenty-Four

"I guess today is the day, man. You gonna be out of there for a period of time, terrorizing the women of Cali before your girl gets there. Man, they are not gonna know what hit'em." Issac laughed heartedly.

"Naw, man, it ain't even gonna be like that. I plan to be too busy with trying to learn all I have to learn, opening the new club and finding a place for me and Melanie. I can't put her in just any place I have to find a house, not an apartment. I've been looking online at some houses. Shit, houses out there can break a man; have you working day and night; I wanna be able to enjoy life and enjoy it with Mel, not leave her alone a lot because I'm working to pay for some over-priced house."

"She'll be working too, right? The two incomes should be okay."

"Yeah, she'll be working but I don't want her to spend all her time at work either, I want her with me. We are a couple."

"Damn, you just sounded like her husband, Kev. There's something deep rooted there you're not saying." He looked at Kevin sideways. "What gives, man? I think I know but to hear it from you is a different story."

Kevin snickered, "Right now it's deep rooted, my man." He patted Issac on the back. "Those feelings will surface when they're ready. In the meantime…"

"I feel ya man, not trying to rush anything."

Chapter Twenty-Five

"Today's the day, babe. Are you ready to make our final move?"

Kevin had been back and forth to California getting acquainted with his new job at Lowe Enterprises and finding a house for he and Melanie to make a home. Melanie joined him on a few occasions to get familiar with her new job as well and to decorate the new house. Not only did they decorate the house, they christened almost every room within the house. They wanted to leave one room untouched until their first official and final move in day.

"I'm all packed and ready to go. I'm glad we're not driving I'm exhausted from this last bit of packing. Our last trip filled up both of our cars, we should have hired movers."

"Yeah, just for your clothes alone. Woman, I'm glad we have a large walk in closet, just for you. Now, time to get to the airport. The shuttle is here."

"I'm making sure everything is locked up, Mina can be forgetful and leave a window open."

***

On the plane Kevin wanted so much to pull Melanie into the bathroom but thought against the idea. The memory of the flight he met Rhonda on came to mind. Immediately he dismissed the idea. He thought more highly of Melanie.

Melanie's thoughts were all over the place; she was wondering if she was doing the right thing, after all, she has only known Kevin for five months.

"What if our relationship doesn't work out? What if he turns out not to be the person I see before me now? Dammit, why didn't I think of these things earlier? I've never made a move like this before, and especially with a man. And one I hadn't known for long. I'm doing it now, no turning back. I'm going to give the relationship the benefit of the doubt and think positive. I'm already making the move and I'm going forward. If he acts a fool...heaven help him," she thought to herself.

"Earth to Melanie! Say babe, where were you? You seemed miles away. Come back to me. Don't let me lose you now."

"I'm sorry Sweetie. I had drifted for a moment. Thinking about this new move and where it's going to take us."

"Not having second thoughts, I hope. Let me know before this plane gets off the ground. I want you with me. I want us to be together." Kevin said, squeezing Melanie's hand.

"No second thoughts. I'm good." She leaned over to give Kevin a small kiss on his lips.

"Good. I was getting nervous for a minute there. You know how to scare a man. What are you reading? That same book you started a while back?"

"Yes, it's *'Intimate Moments' by Jeané Sashi*. I hadn't had the chance to finish it with being busy with you and the move. Not that I'm complaining or anything but this is a good book. I'm enjoying reading it. The main character is something else. But, the bottom line is, she's just looking for love and to be loved."

"Sounds interesting, I may have to read it after you finish it," Kevin replied resting his head on the headrest and closing his eyes.

Chapter Twenty-Six

In L.A., they were picked up by a waiting car. Super Shuttle sent a Lincoln Town car to pick them up as opposed to the regular Big Blue Van with other passengers aboard. This was an exclusive, just for Melanie and Kevin. Kevin arranged this. He didn't want Melanie to have to wait, nor did he want her to have to share seating with anyone else. Plus, he wanted her all to himself. Maybe he could ravish her in the backseat of the car.

Riding through the L.A. traffic from the airport was exciting for both Melanie and Kevin. They knew this was it… no turning back, now. Kevin putting his hand on Melanie's right thigh, he could feel her trembling through her thigh. "What's wrong? I can tell you're nervous. Don't be, I'm right here and I'm not going anywhere. I've found what I've been looking for in you and I'm not going anywhere, rest assured on that. You're going to have to kill me to get me away from you." They both laughed.

"Kill you? That extreme, huh? I'm just a little nervous. This is surreal and change such as this should make anyone nervous. But, I'm okay."

"I love you Melanie. I didn't think I would say those words ever again but that's the way I feel and not just right now. I've been feeling them for a while now. I hope you understand how I feel. That's why I said that I'm not going anywhere. I'm in love with you." Melanie was shocked that those words came out of his mouth. Kevin couldn't pull them back if he wanted to. He was also relieved.

"I'm surprised you told me you love me. I've been trying to figure out a way to say the same thing to you. I knew I wouldn't have made this move if I didn't love you or was in love with you. Everything happened so fast, I couldn't believe it. It feels good to have those feelings finally out in the open. Now, I know everything is going to be good. I feel better now."

***

"We're here! Home Sweet Home!" Kevin exclaimed excitedly.

The driver got their suitcases out of the trunk and took them to their front door. Kevin already had Melanie in his arms carrying her over the threshold as if they had just gotten married.

"Put me down, I can walk." Melanie kicked her stiletto heeled feet.

"I know you can walk, maybe I'm practicing, ever thought about that?"

"Practicing? Hmmm. No comment."

Both were standing in the foyer of their new home looking around. They both couldn't believe they made it and their new beginning was just beginning. They stood side by side holding hands just looking around. There was nothing to be done in the house as Melanie had done all the decorating and everything was already in its place. Looking at their accomplishments, they both couldn't help but smile.

"Are you ready for what lies ahead of us? I know I'm ready." Kevin asked.

"I'm ready. I'm looking forward to this new journey."

"In that case," Kevin stood directly in front of Melanie and took her hands into his. "Melanie, I know it's been a short time that we've known each other you've enlightened me to that but I feel I have known you for a very long time…years to be exact." Kevin's hands were trembling but he was confident. "I want us to be together for a very long time, like the rest of our lives. What I'm trying to ask you Mel," Kevin knelt and asked. "Will you marry me? Be my wife, my life partner, you're already my friend. Be my helpmate. You've already calmed me down and have me somewhat tamed. How about keeping me that way? Be in my life forever?" Kevin came out of his pocket with a gorgeous 3-carat, heart shaped platinum engagement ring.

Melanie with tear filled eyes running down her face smiled showing her right dimple answers Kevin with "Yes, I will marry you." Threw her arms around his neck while he was still on bended knee and planted a kiss on the top of his head, then his forehead and bent further to kiss Kevin's lips. That kiss led to lovemaking right in the foyer, near the front door with it wide open for all to see.

Looking into each other eyes and feeling the love that has transpired between them. The heat in their bodies started to rise causing them to want each other evermore. Kevin kissed Melanie passionately as if his world was coming to an end. His hands roamed her body stopping at her breast. He squeezed her left breast gently while still exploring her mouth with his tongue. He was so hot for his fiancée he couldn't contain himself. His right hand found its way under her blouse and under her lace bra. There he felt the flesh of her breast, this caused him to become more heated, wanting her more. He unhooked her bra as she was unbuttoning her blouse.

Melanie wanted Kevin as much as he wanted her. She was now topless and panting. Kevin took off his shirt and met her with being topless. He knelt down to kiss her and lowered his head to her right breast. His tongue circled her areola before his mouth began to devour the dime sized nipple. He cupped her breast to make sure he took her all into his mouth. He was sucking on her breast the way a baby sucked on his mother's breast for milk. He was not letting go, all the while fondling and squeezing her left breast with his right hand. Melanie is kissing Kevin on his neck and moaning in his ear, "I want you so bad...let me feel you. Let us cum together." She said nothing but words to Kevin, before she knew it, Kevin had them both out of their clothes. She closed her eyes and laid back on the carpeted floor to let Kevin have his way.

It wasn't long before he was down south on her body. He was devouring her as if she was his last meal. He sucked on her thighs, lapped at the lips of her vagina before reaching her clit and taking it between his teeth to let his tongue work it over to drive her crazy. As his tongue was working her clit over, Melanie was working her hips putting all of her in his face, making sure Kevin didn't miss anything. She wiggled and bucked until she came as hard as she's ever come before. He sucked up all her juices as though he was sucking the last bit of ice cream out of a push-up pop. He didn't want to waste a drop. He couldn't wait to enter her, let her feel how hard he was for her, consummate their engagement. Kevin's manhood was jumping are like it was a wand...it wouldn't keep still. He wanted to be inside of Melanie so bad. Coming up to lay his body on top of hers, his rod found its own way inside of her through her open legs and waiting wetness.

Feeling how wet she was only told him how much she wanted him. Making him believe she meant what she said about loving him. Feeling her wetness and her arms wrapped around him along with her legs brought tears to his eyes. He was so in love with her. Thrusting his love into her, he wanted her to feel all of him. He wanted her to know that he really loved her. If he could, he would put his whole body inside of her. With his arms wrapped around her body and her arms wrapped around his body, it would take the Jaws of Life to pry them apart. With the lovemaking they were doing, Melanie had a nice, wet puddle under her. They were going to have to get that section of the carpet cleaned.

"Kevin, baby, I can't hold it any longer. I'm going to bust. You're going to make me scream."

"Go ahead and scream baby," He whispered in her ear. "We're at home, in our home. I'm going to cum with you. Cum with me."

"I'm cuming Kevin, it's all yours, take it. I love you!"

"We're in sync. I love you too baby! Oh my God, it's coming. Damn you feel so good!"

Lying wrapped in exhaustion, panting from the quick lovemaking that just took place, both Melanie and Kevin fall asleep quick in each other's arms not caring where they are. Their beginning had just begun.

Chapter Twenty-Seven

Kevin spent the day in his new office, in meetings and speaking with Issac via telephone. He had settled in his new position just fine.

"Kevin, you haven't missed a beat with coming to L.A. to run the clubs...we like this." Reggie took notice. "To be honest man, I thought this transition was going to take some time getting used to. But, you've proved me wrong."

"Why do you say that, Mr. Lowe? I feel I adjust pretty well."

"It seemed you were pretty comfortable in New Orleans. There was nothing wrong with that. I know how that is. I was comfortable in San Diego until I made the move back the L.A., at least to the Rancho Cucamonga area. A good woman would do that to you."

"Yes, she sure will."

"Have the two of you settled in as of yet? How does she, Melanie, right, like the house?"

"Melanie, that's correct. She loves the house and her new job. We've settled in just fine. Thank you."

"That's cool. Maybe the four of us Me, Tonju, You and Melanie, can get together and have dinner sometime soon. We would like to get to know her as well and show the both of you

L.A. as well as take the both of you out on our boat."

"We would like that. We haven't done much since we've been here with both of us getting right into our new jobs."

"It's a deal. I'll speak to Tonju about it and get back to you."

"Sounds good boss."

"I'll let you get back to work. You're doing a great job." Reggie left Kevin's office.

***

Kevin answered the phone in his office, "This is Kevin Stokes."

"Hey Kev man, how you doing?" asked Issac.

"What's up Issac, man? I'm doing great and you? What do I owe the pleasure of this call? Twice in one day."

"Well, man, I'm not one to gossip and you know this but I thought I would tell you. That loud mouth girl, what's her name? Oh Rhonda, ole girl went and got herself married. She came in here sporting her ring. She said she couldn't wait on you to come to your senses any longer. She married some guy she met after you left the first time and had only known for about three weeks. Dude barely has any teeth and no job. I guess she likes charity cases," Issac rolled with laughter.

"Damn charity cases. I guess I was a charity case to her for a minute but I wasn't willing to marry her ass. Well, at least she found someone to give her what I refused to give her. I hope she's happy. I wish her much luck."

"She bought her own wedding ring. Now how crazy is that?" Issac said still laughing so hard he was damn near choking.

"She wanted to be married that bad. How are you a Mina doing? I know Mel spoke with her a few days ago but I didn't ask her anything about the conversation."

"We're doing great! I'm so into that girl it's not funny. Yeah, she got a brother wrapped around her finger. She told me congratulations are in order for you and Mel. Congrats man, when is the big day?"

"Thank you man. We haven't set a date yet. We've both been busy with our jobs, but when we do, you and Mina will be the first to know. And the two of you will be next or before us if we don't set a date. I don't think you're letting Mina go." Kevin said busting out laughing.

"You got that right. That woman ain't going anywhere. Not if I can help it. Keep us posted man. Let me get back to work. I'll holla at you soon. Tell Melanie hi from us."

"Will do man. Take care."

***

"Kevin, we need you to get down to the club on Wilshire. There seems to be a problem with an employee there." Tonju peeked in his office and gave him the directive.

"I wonder what the problem is. I'll go right now. Thanks Tonju."

Chapter Twenty-Eight

Kevin walked into the club, it was four o'clock in the afternoon and the club didn't open for another five hours. "What the hell is going on in here? I don't see anyone. Hey, is anyone here?" Kevin called out across the club.

"We're in here." someone called back and Kevin didn't recognize the voice.

The voice was coming from the store room. Kevin walked in that direction only to be met by the manager of the club who Kevin hired on his first trip out to L.A.

"What's going on man? Why was I told to come out here?"

"Man, we have a big problem. When I came in a couple of hours ago, I found this woman in the storeroom crying."

"Woman? What woman? And crying? What's going on?"

"She said one of the bartenders locked her in the storeroom after he raped her."

"What the fuck?! Are you kidding me? I don't need this shit right now and neither does the owners? Who in the fuck is the bartender? Get me his name now! Better yet, get all the employees in here, NOW! Let them know, if they don't get down here, they will be fired right over the phone!"

"Yes, sir. I'll call everyone in."

***

The employees had been summoned and all have arrived and were standing before Kevin who was now pissed beyond compare.

"Who in the hell locked this woman in the storeroom and on top of that raped her? Don't everyone answer all at once, but I want an answer, preferably from the person who did this shit."

Everyone looked around at each other, from person to person. Some were looking confused and some knew but wouldn't tell.

"If no one answers, I will fire all of you right on the spot and hire new people within the hour, how about that? I don't have time to waste, so quit wasting my time."

With that comment the employees started to become uncomfortable. One employee stepped up.

"Mr. Stokes, it was me. I don't know if I should apologize to her or not but I will apologize to you. She was coming on to me last night and when we closed the club, she was still here. She came out of the bathroom half naked. I asked her to leave and she followed me into the storeroom. She started flirting and rubbing her body against mine and when I started to respond to her she really tried to play hard to get. That's when I pushed her up against a wall and gave it to her. When we were through, she said she was going to call the police and say that I raped her. That's when I locked her in the storeroom. I was going to let her out tonight when the crowd got here. It would have been her word against mine. She's a tease and a hoe."

"Well, I'm glad you were honest with me and told me the whole story, I think." Kevin then turned to the Manager, "Get her out of here. Make sure she gets home okay. I'll handle it from here."

The other employees were standing in a Military style line scared to death of what was coming next. They were in disbelief of what just unfolded and how Kevin was going to handle it.

"Do you think you did the right thing, son? I mean by raping her and locking her in the storeroom?"

"She wanted it and I didn't want her to tell anyone."

"You're a cocky son of a bitch." With that statement, Kevin held off and busted the employee right in the mouth drawing blood. From that point on, Kevin commenced to whooping his ass while the other employees watched. A female employee called the police from her cell phone. Kevin wouldn't let up on the man. He was pissed and angry. All of his rage came flooding out. While Kevin was beating the man senseless, he was telling him "I don't condone rape, nor being held hostage. It takes a sick motherfucker to do something like that. I will make you pay. She didn't deserve that I don't care how she came on to you." By this time, the man was bleeding profusely from his mouth and his nose.

***

The police arrived and saw Kevin beating the man's ass. No one stepped in to stop the royal ass whooping that Kevin was instilling on this man. They were too scared after witnessing the look on Kevin's face.

"Sir, stop what you're doing and step away from that man," ordered one officer with his gun drawn. Another officer hurried over to where the commotion was and began trying to pull Kevin off his employee. He succeeded and handcuffed Kevin as well. They pulled the man off the floor and called for an ambulance…he was that badly beaten.

"Can someone tell us what happened here?" The officer asked while putting his revolver back into its holster.

One of the waitresses spoke up, "Mr. Stokes beat the hell out of Jarrod because we all just found out that Jarrod raped a guest of the club last night and locked her in the storeroom overnight."

"Who found the woman?" asked the officer.

"Our Manager, I believe. He just took her home to make sure she was okay."

"Did anyone get the woman's name or have any information on her?"

"Yes, I have her name, address and telephone number," responded Gary, the manager, walking back into the club. "She said if you want to contact her, she is willing to give a statement."

"That we will do. But, in the meantime, we will have to take you into custody for assault," one of the offices said addressing Kevin.

"Are you kidding me? He was defending the woman's honor. This is a joke," stated the waitress.

"Gary, do me a favor and call the corporate office and ask to speak to Mr. Lowe. Tell him what transpired here and let him know that I've been arrested. Don't leave anything out. Ask them to call my fiancée to let her know what's going on. Then have them call my attorney, Mr. Tony Greer, in Chicago. His phone number is listed. Do that in the order I just gave you."

"Okay, will do, but you know this is some bullshit! That piece of shit commits rape and you get carted off to jail? Where's the justice in that?"

Chapter Twenty-Nine

Melanie arrived at the Police Station along with Tonju and Reggie. "What is going on here, why are you holding my fiancée? From what we were told, he was defending the honor of one of his female patrons."

"Ma'am, the man he almost beat unconscious is pressing charges against him. In the meantime, we are booking him and transporting him to the County Jail. If the D.A. doesn't pick up the case within seventy-two hours, he will be released. Meaning all charges will be dropped," the officer informed the trio.

"I know about 'charges' and how they work," Tonju informed the officer. I'm an Attorney. Mr. Stokes' attorney will be here this evening. When will he be transported?

"We will be transporting him within the hour, Ma'am."

"Can we see him?" asked Tonju.

"Sure. One moment," answered the officer.

***

Kevin sat in a holding cell with his head in his hands not believing that he was back in this hell hole again. Thinking to himself...his damn temper. He was hoping this mess didn't cause him to lose Melanie or his job.

"Kevin, honey, thank God you're alright. You're going to

get out of this mess," stated Melanie with tears in her eyes through the glass that was separating them.

"Baby, I'm fine, just mad as hell, that's all."

"Kevin, we've called Mr. Greer and he will be here this evening. In the meantime, they're transporting you to the County Jail for booking. It appears the man you beat up is pressing charges against you. By the way, I didn't know you knew Tony Greer. He's a colleague of mine. We worked on a previous case together. He's a very good attorney," Tonju chimed in over Melanie's shoulder.

From Tonju's left side, "Man, you took flight on that dude. He's messed up. But, in all honesty, he deserved it. The woman is going to press charges against him, so I guess this is going to get interesting. But, you will be out of here soon."

"Baby, Mr. Greer told us not to bail you out. He will handle everything when he gets here and that you will be out of here tonight. Baby, I'm scared, what if he doesn't get you out?"

"Mel, don't worry, when Mr. Greer says he's going to do something, you best believe he's going to do it. Just trust him…I do."

"He's right Melanie, Tony is a sharp shooter. This will all be over before it begins," Tonju reassured Melanie.

"Ok, I'll trust him. I just want my baby home where he belongs."

"I'll be there soon enough, sweetie and our life will pick up right where we left off. And rest assured, you will be my wife soon enough. We're not only a couple; we're a pair and a team. So go home and on the way, get some of those wedding books and start planning our wedding. Or hire one of those wedding planners. We are going to do this and I mean it."

Chapter Thirty

"That motherfucker is going to pay for what he did to me. I'm going to make sure that he goes to jail for a long time with his self-righteous ass." Jarrod looked at himself in the mirror from his hospital bed.

"That bitch deserved what she got. They all do. They shouldn't come in the club looking like they do and dressing the way they do and not expect someone to say anything to them. I'm going to make sure the D.A. picks this case up. He just got the job so I know he can't afford an attorney so a senseless P.D. will pick up the case and not know what he's doing he will lose or make him plead out," Jarrod said laughing to himself in the mirror.

Not only did Jarrod not know that Kevin did have an attorney but his attorney was on his way to L.A. in his hour of cockiness. And the woman that he raped was going to press charges, so his world might get turned upside down. He might not have time to even blink.

***

Just as Kevin was being transport to the County Jail, Mr. Greer was making his connecting flight in Houston, Texas on his way to Los Angeles, California. By the time Kevin was booked into County Jail, Mr. Greer's plane would be landing.

"Hi Tony nice to see you again. Sorry it has to be under these circumstances," Tonju greeted Tony as he entered her law office.

"Hi Tonju good to see you again as well. You can brief me on the way to County Jail as to what exactly happened. My rental car is in the parking lot. I know Mr. Stokes and he can have temper but something detriment had to have happened for him to have beat that man that bad."

"True, it was a bad thing that happened and Kevin was just defending someone and got pissed at the same time."

"I've already notified the Judge, he'll be meeting us there."

"You don't waste any time. I see you're still the same…go for the win. There we're alike."

"I've seen you in action and you're a pit bull in stilettos. You have a bite on you lady."

"Here we are. Let's go get him."

"They won't know what hit'em."

***

"Judge Stevenson, how are you Sir? I'm glad you could meet me on such short notice."

"I'm doing well, Mr. Greer. This sounded too messy to pass up. Mrs. Lowe, how are you? Looks like that baby is ready to pop out of there."

"Nice to see you too Judge Stevenson. Yes, I'm due in two months, we can't wait."

"Good, good. Mr. Greer, Mrs. Lowe briefed me on this case and the defendant has a butt load of witnesses, so this should be a closed case."

"My thoughts exactly, Judge."

"Well, let's go get him out."

Standing at the reception counter of the County Jail waiting to see the Superintendent, there are people everywhere. Women were coming to visit their men in jail and babies crying all over the place.

"Superintendent Harris, good to see you. We need to go into your office and talk," Judge Stevenson addressed the Superintendent.

"It's good to see you too Judge. This must be really important to bring you down here at this time of the evening and to have an entouragé with you."

"It is serious. These are attorney's Mrs. Lowe and Mr. Greer. They're here on the matter at hand as well."

"Nice to meet both of you."

"You too," Tonju and Tony replied in unisom.

Sitting in the Superintendent's office the Judge led the conversation. He got straight to the point.

"Harris, a man was just booked in here and he shouldn't have been arrested at all but unfortunately, we have a few arrest eager police officers bucking to try to prove something to someone. The officers failed to hear the entire story before taking the man into custody. Here's the entire story," the Judge looked at and motioned towards Tonju.

Tonju told the Superintendent the entire story and the look on his face looked as if he was going to throw up. He was in disbelief by the time she finished telling him everything. She told him that the woman had already pressed rape and kidnapping charges against the man. She also informed him that the police should have him handcuffed to his hospital bed as they were speaking and they jumped real quickly on this case to beat the D.A.

"So you can see where we are with this Superintendent Harris," interjected Tony. "I'm the defendant's attorney and flew out here to get him released and I plan on accomplishing that tonight. My client did nothing wrong."

"Mr. Greer, I see you're passionate about this but I can't promise you anything. However, you can bond your client out."

"Bond him out? That won't happen. I won't bond out an innocent man. He 'will' walk out of here without being bonded."

"Calm down, Tony. As you can see Harris, Mr. Greer means business. Mrs. Lowe is his employer and they're here in support of him. As Mr. Greer states, the defendant will be released without bond," stated Judge Stevenson.

"I can't just let an inmate out of here without a court order, you know that Judge."

"I take it you're not too bright, Mr. Harris. What do you think the Judge is here for?" commented Tonju.

"You mean Judge you have orders to release him? I didn't think of that."

"I see you didn't," stated Tonju.

"Yes, Harris," the Judge laid the court order in front of him on his desk. "The defendant or inmate as you call him is to be released right now. We'll wait."

Superintendent Harris got up out of his chair and walked from behind his desk. He couldn't believe his ears. In all of his days as Superintendent, a Judge has not released an inmate without the inmate being before him in the courtroom. He summoned a guard to go get Kevin and bring him to his office.

Kevin walked in the Superintendent's office with a blank look on his face. Once he saw Tonju and his attorney, Tony Greer. He smiled but became confused when he saw the other gentleman that he did not know or recognize.

"Have a seat Mr. Stokes. I summonsed you for a reason. I take it you know Mrs. Lowe and Mr. Greer? This gentleman is Judge Stevenson…"

"Hello...Judge Stevenson." Kevin greeted the Judge looking apprehensive.

"Hey Kevin."

"Kevin, its good seeing you again but not under these circumstances," state Tony Greer.

"Hello Mrs. Lowe, Mr. Greer."

"Kevin, we're going to get right to the point. Mrs. Lowe and Mr. Greer have gone to bat for you and have gone to great lengths to get you released from jail. They even got the Judge involved in this case. The judge brought the court order himself to have you released. You have some heavy hitters believing in you. With that being said you are free to go home."

"Will the charges be dropped or is that guy still pressing charges?"

"You can rest assured the charges will be dropped," answered Tonju.

"Who bailed me out and how much was it so I can pay it back?"

"There was no bail. You're walking free," replied the Judge.

Kevin looked like he was going to cry and began thanking everyone and gave Tonju a hug. He was anxious to get home to Melanie.

He walked out of the Superintendent's office and into the waiting room of the jail Melanie ran up and wrapped her arms around Kevin.

"Baby, I'm so glad you're alright and I'm taking you home where you belong."

"Who told you I was being released? I just found out and didn't have a chance to call you."

"I did Kevin. I sent a text to Reggie and told him to get in touch with Melanie and have her get down here as soon as possible."

"You guys do work fast."

"When did you text your husband, Tonju? I didn't see that and I was sitting right next to you," inquired Tony.

"Don't fret, I'm as good as you are Tony."

"Well, I don't care when it was done, I'm glad it was done and I have my baby here with me now," Melanie chimed in.

"I second that," Kevin raised his hand. "Now, I can go home, be with my honey and do what we do best." He winked at Melanie.

"Kevin, have a good night." closed Tonju and Tony.

EXCERPT FROM
Check-Mate
BY Jeané Sashi

Introduction

"This is a place I really don't want to be in. How could I have let this happen? Twenty-five to Life. That Judge was not playing; all because my temper had got the best of me. But, then again, dude jumped on me. Now, look at me, I'm sitting here in this damn hell hole."

As he sat in his cell he listened to all the camaraderie from the other cells. Terrell was pissed that this has happened to him. He thought he was only going to be in the County Jail for a short time but so far it felt like a lift-time. He couldn't even hear himself think half of the time. And let us not mention the food. It's not fit for human consumption.

"Man, I had no intention of being a part of the rainbow coalition we call jail. Who was it that said collateral damage is like jail; there's always room for more?" I don't like being a part of this damn 'more'. And to top it all off, my girl is pregnant. Damn!"

I'm gonna take advantage of some counseling while I do this time. I've got to get a handle on my temper. In the meantime, my attorney said she's gonna appeal this case. I won't hold my breath but, I hope she does. While the appeal is going on, I'm sitting here in this County Jail."

Terrell was deep in thought and didn't hear his cell door open. He was getting a new cell mate.

"What's up man?" Kevin entered the cell with his belongings. "Guess I'm your new celly. Not looking to be here long. Looks like I have the top bunk."

"Yeah, the top bunk is all yours. How long you got?"

"Hopefully, I'll be outta here in the next day or two. My attorney is working on this shit. A case is not a good thing to have when you're trying to start over with your life. My girl and I came out here to Cali with new jobs, to start our lives as a couple, and to have some fun and this shit happens." Kevin shook his head. "My girl is all worried and we just bought a new house here in L.A."

"Damn, man, sound like you had it going on and got caught up. That ain't cool." Terrell commented.

"Yeah, but I have a damn good Attorney, so I'm looking to being the fuck out of here like yesterday. Why is it that some people just want to take the chance to ice skate uphill? I just don't get it."

"I know what you mean, man. My temper made me check this fool and that's how I landed here. I have to get my temper in check."

"You have a temper too? I guess we both could use some anger management," Kevin laughed at the thought.

"Yeah, my anger made me crack this dude's skull. Split his head wide open. I'm looking at twenty-five man. I hope my attorney is as good as you say yours is. She seems cool, though. And she knows her shit."

"Good luck to you, man. That's some time you're facing."

"Tell me about it."

The clatter of keys was walking down the corridor and slowly approaching the cell where Kevin was being housed. Terrell was thinking, "Someone is getting out, I guess. I wish it were me."

"Stokes?!" demanded the guard as he was unlocking the cell door. "Come with me, the Superintendent wants to see you. Get all of your belongings."

Kevin looked back at Terrell and wondered what was going on and Terrell shrugged his shoulders.

"What's going on? Why does the Superintendent want to see me? Kevin asked the guard.

"What do I look like, Wikipedia? Just come on."

Kevin thought to himself as he was getting the things he brought into the cell a few moments ago, "Rude motherfucker. I guess he's not happy with his job."

Kevin arrived at the Superintendent's office, walked in and saw Tonju, Mr. Greer and a man he did not recognize along with Superintendent Harris.

Be on the lookout for the rest of the author's third novel.

About the Author

A Former Corporate Mortgage employee, Jeané Sashi is also a college graduate. After several years into her career, Jeané figured out that the Corporate America life wasn't for her. Needing an outlet for her energy, that was growing creatively, she left the Corporate World and began to seek out other creative avenues, She pulled out some erotic stories she had written, but kept hidden for years, and is now beginning to let them manifest into written novels.

http://www.JeaneEBennett.com

Would you like to see your manuscript become a book?

If you are interested in becoming a PublishAmerica author, please submit your manuscript for possible publication to us at:

acquisitions@publishamerica.com

You may also mail in your manuscript to:

**PublishAmerica
PO Box 151
Frederick, MD 21705**

We also offer free graphics for Children's Picture Books!

---

www.publishamerica.com

CPSIA information can be obtained at www.ICGtesting.com
Printed in the USA
LVOW06s0752270713

344875LV00001B/36/P